"I can't go out with you."

"So we don't go out. We don't have dinner." Warren's arm unfolded across the back of the couch until Tabitha could feel the heat of his skin close to her shoulders, his hand coming to rest lightly on the back of her head, fingers sifting gently through the ends of her hair until her scalp tingled pleasantly.

And that wasn't the only tingle.

Her eyelids grew heavy at the hypnotic brush of his fingers through her hair, the solid male presence of him beside her urging her to lean on him, into him, all over him.

Oh, that sounded unwise. And tempting.

"What do you want?" Warren prompted.

She was tongue-tied and turned on.

"I'll tell you what *I* want," he said. "I want to kiss you. Thoroughly. Let me do that."

"You're consulting me?" Her fingers reached up to touch the open collar of his shirt. "I'm very much in favor of kissing."

Blaze™

Dear Reader,

For writers, inspiration can come from all kinds of crazy places. When I was ready to follow up *Don't Look Back* (Harlequin Blaze, February 2007), I knew I wanted another steamy suspense with an edge of danger and I already had a fantastic hero ready and waiting. But what to do about a heroine?

Days passed while I thought about it and then I spotted an ad for *Pretty Woman*. For some reason, I remembered that Julia Roberts had a body double for that movie and I wondered what it would be like to own a gorgeous pair of legs and not to get full credit for them when they appeared on billboards around the world. And bingo! Just like that, in walked Tabitha Everheart, who has not been given enough credit in her life either, but she was ready to change the problem once I got her story underway.

I hope you'll enjoy *Just One Look* and Tabitha's decision to take a walk on the steamy side of life. Please visit me anytime on the Harlequin Blaze message boards at eHarlequin.com or at www.joannerock.com to learn more about my books.

Happy reading!

Joanne Rock

JUST ONE LOOK

Joanne Rock

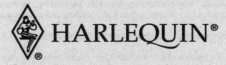

TORONTO • NEW YORK • LONDON
AMSTERDAM • PARIS • SYDNEY • HAMBURG
STOCKHOLM • ATHENS • TOKYO • MILAN • MADRID
PRAGUE • WARSAW • BUDAPEST • AUCKLAND

ISBN-13: 978-0-373-79315-0
ISBN-10:   0-373-79315-4

JUST ONE LOOK

www.eHarlequin.com

Printed in U.S.A.

ABOUT THE AUTHOR

From *To Catch a Thief* to *Body Heat* and *The Big Easy*, RITA® Award-nominated author Joanne Rock loves a sexy suspense story where the hero and heroine aren't quite sure how far to trust one another. Her thirst for writing a wide range of stories has revisited this theme in both modern and medieval tales alike. Her books have been reprinted in twenty-two countries and translated into sixteen languages. A former college teacher and public relations coordinator, she has a master's degree in English from the University of Louisville and started writing when she became a stay-at-home mom. Learn more about Joanne and her work by visiting her at www.joannerock.com.

Books by Joanne Rock

Don't miss any of our special offers. Write to us at the following address for information on our newest releases.

Harlequin Reader Service
U.S.: 3010 Walden Ave., P.O. Box 1325, Buffalo, NY 14269
Canadian: P.O. Box 609, Fort Erie, Ont. L2A 5X3

To Bernice Rock,
the best mother-in-law in the whole world.
Thank you for all the great dinners, the moral
support and the many times you've watched the
boys so I could attend writer conferences or go
out on a date with your son. I would have never
gotten my porch painted without you!

Prologue

RED TOOK GREAT PLEASURE from hiding in plain sight.

The assistant producer mingled with the B-movie star's entourage, an invitation to another studio's set never difficult to procure if you had connections.

God bless connections. In New York's underground film industry, you could buy your way to the top faster with the right contacts than you could with a big schlong or double D boobs. And while Red might not have the kind of star power that dingbat John de Milo possessed in the industry, at least Red knew how to make friends and blend in on the bedroom set of a cable after-dark special that wasn't quite porn but wouldn't make the cut as an R-rated movie. In a business full of insecurity, appearing non-threatening to all egomaniac parties concerned was critical to longevity. That fine art of flying under the radar helped when it came to treading the outside borders of what was legal in filmmaking. Plus, the anonymity allowed Red to lurk right underneath Tabitha Everhart's nose.

"Quiet on the set," the director called to calm the din of the crowd in a studio that had more of a party atmosphere than any Hollywood production.

Actor John de Milo was the last one to shut his trap, but then he looked like he was tripping on the sidelines of the set—not a good thing for a man who'd been privy to sensitive information once upon a time. Red would have to do something about that.

Tabitha Everhart hadn't opened her mouth all day, her visit to the set where she'd been hired to act as a body double next week just a chance to observe the filming in action. But just because Tabitha was quiet today didn't mean she would be forever. Tabitha was one of very few people who had all the necessary pieces to uncover Red's secrets.

"Action!" The director's call started the sex scene in motion and the bedroom backdrop became a playground for the three so-called actors intent on using the cable movie for a jump to more legitimate shows.

This was the upscale version of porn? Red's producer's eye took a jaundiced view of a piece that wouldn't make nearly as much as something spicier.

If only Tabitha had consented to making that erotic film long ago. She would have been one of the industry's stars and she'd never be hungry for work again. Her high-profile divorce wouldn't have hurt the kind of career she could have had. As it was, Tabitha struggled financially.

A damn shame she had missed such an opportunity. And an even bigger shame that she knew too much. There was an old-school sweetness about Tabitha that everyone admired—even her egomaniac colleagues. In this business, that was saying something.

The actors moaned and sighed over one another as they bent over the bed without really taking off anything substantial yet, their bodies just needed for close ups of skin and lips, closed eyelids and scratching fingernails. But the sexual pantomime continued for an audience of at least twenty-five, with John de Milo acting out an exaggerated version of the male star's hip-driving thrusts in the shadows of the set well behind the director.

Tabitha ignored the guy, studiously observing the scene in front of her rather than acknowledging the actor's dry-humping technique. Red suspected she'd flee the set as soon as the director called cut.

Then Red would be back to following her more discreetly. No more hiding in plain sight.

Because no matter that Tabitha didn't realize she'd walked away with a key piece of information about Red during her divorce, the body double would have to be silenced.

1

KEEPING A CLOSE REIN on his dog's leash, Warren Vitalis rounded the corner of Bank Street and Greenwich Avenue with the same wary alertness of any cop who'd been on the job for at least a decade. Around every bend lurked the possibility of danger, even for an off-duty detective out taking his mutt for a run.

"Hi, Warren." Two middle-aged men strolling down Bank Street arm in arm greeted Warren instead of any danger.

"You guys are done early," Warren shouted back as he sped past the partners who shared ownership of a restaurant and an antique store on the route Warren and Buster ran every night. "Is business slow?"

"Bite your tongue, Detective," the slighter man—Scott—called back. "We just hired help to close up at night so we can turn in early. We're not the party boys we used to be."

Warren flashed a thumbs-up before gaining speed through a construction zone where the street was covered by a temporary wooden tunnel. Notorious places for crime, the passageways provided plenty of nooks for thieves to hide, but Buster didn't look worried. The Akida-German shepherd mix charged into the darkness with typical speed. Warren might not be on duty tonight and he wasn't in his own precinct, but he still considered this section of the West Village to be his beat since he lived a couple of blocks over. If he could provide a little extra safety for Scott and DeShaun, the restaurateurs, or for the handful of people who were out for a walk at 11:00 p.m., he felt a little more worthy of his badge.

Either that, or maybe riding a desk at the precinct for half his shift hours lately simply made him itchy to be back on the streets. His ballistics expertise had made for a fast career rise after a rough start, but it had also tied him to cold case files more often than he cared to remember. As rewarding as it might be to catch a perp roaming free ten years after the guy committed his crime, Warren missed the adrenaline rush that came with working cases in progress.

Slowing down at a shuffling noise between the scaffolding posts inside the construction tunnel, he spotted a homeless guy catching a few z's on a length of cardboard. Buster circled back to stand by Warren's legs, vigilant even when the threat level was low.

"Hey, Larry." In his twelve years on the force, Warren had learned you couldn't save every homeless guy on the street. That didn't stop him from at least recognizing them, since one of the biggest threats to a vagrant's already tenuous grip on their pride was fading from the public consciousness all together. If society refused to see these people, sooner or later they vanished.

There was a time in Warren's life where he'd identified more than Larry would ever know.

"Larry?"

Warren started to lean down to make sure the guy was still breathing at the same time Buster's ears straightened. A low growl started in the dog's throat, but the warning wasn't directed toward the drunk passed out with a bottle of Night Train still clutched in one hand. Buster's sudden wariness was focused at the far end of the construction tunnel.

Straightening, Warren listened to the night noises outside the thin plywood walls that housed the laborers from cold winter winds whipping past. Cars rushing by, tires clunking over maintenance hole covers, and the music from a nearby bar were all the usual sounds of this block.

Until a shot fired.

Sprinting toward the echo the same time as his dog, Warren raced headlong through the tunnel, past endless scaffolding and walls that prevented a clear sight of the street. Tires squealed outside as a car took off, but by the time he emerged from the Gotham City passageway, the vehicle must have already turned up Hudson or a road farther down.

He would have followed his sense of hearing to chase a potential license plate, his pace as fast as any detective in the city thanks to numerous Ironman competitions over the years, but already he could hear a woman screaming from a building nearby.

Déjà vu.

It was the worst night of his life all over again.

LONG, FROZEN MINUTES passed before Tabitha Everhart could take a breath. In reality it had probably only been half a minute. The shriek of squealing tires had faded to the normal rush of late-night traffic outside her street-level living room window. The methodic thump of cars flying over a maintenance hole cover echoed the erratic beat of her heart in the aftermath of the shot that had pierced her window, shattering it in a vast network of cracks that radiated out from one perfectly round hole in the window.

Time seemed suspended, her gaze locked on the horrible glass spiderweb that meant her world wasn't nearly as safe a she'd been hoping.

"Police. Open up!"

The pounding at the door rattled its way through her momentary daze, startling up full-blown panic. If the police were at her door, wouldn't she have heard sirens? Seen a flashing light outside the broken glass?

Oh, God.

She scrambled toward her phone. Dialed. Fumbled. Dialed again.

The pounding continued. Harder. More ominous.

The man at her door broke through, half falling on the floor in a roll he leaped out of, his gun drawn.

"Has anyone been hit?" He asked the question with the weapon trained on her as his gaze spun around the room.

Words failed her. He was going to shoot her.

She clutched the phone in her hand, her body half sprawled across her coffee table in the race to dial 911.

"I—" Her throat closed. And then the strangest words came to mind despite her fear.

"Since when do the cops point guns at the victims?" Anger at long-ago police officers who'd once shown up at her door for a domestic dispute couldn't help but influence her reaction to this man.

But oh, God, would he answer her stupid question by shooting her?

"Since we have no way of knowing who's a victim and who's a whacked-out killer, ma'am. Warren Vitalis, NYPD." He dug in a back pocket and came up with a leather case that unfolded to show a badge and official-looking identification.

Some of the unreasonable anger fizzled away. Fear returned to weaken her knees.

"May I see?" She kept the phone to her ear and told herself she needed to put 911 on speed dial even though she prayed she'd never have to use it again after tonight.

Her heart still raced from the rush of adrenaline and mind-numbing fear that had robbed her of the ability to remember three simple digits. Nine. One. One.

"Look all you want." He winged over the badge like a Frisbee while he glanced around her humble apartment and makeshift decorating before slowly lowering his gun. "You're alone in the residence?"

She blinked and nodded quickly, a wealth of unexpected emotion suddenly clogging her throat. She ought to know by now that if you suppress your fears long enough they'll come out to bite you in the butt even harder when you're not looking.

Her brain still didn't seem to be functioning as she stared at his identification labeling him as Detective Warren Vitalis of the New York Police Department, true to his word. If she'd only seen his headshot, she would think he looked like a cold, hard man despite the attractive features. He wore his hair so tightly cropped he could have been a marine, the shorn hint of dark hair making him appear dangerous.

A round diamond rested in one ear, moving him more in the category of gangster than military man. She looked up at him now to see the bright white stone wink in the muted streetlight filtering in through sheer curtains that fluttered in the wind now that a hole had been blown through the window.

He studied the broken pattern of the glass for long moments before busting out a pocketsize plastic ruler with a hinge in the middle that allowed it to fold in half. But then she watched him angle the two sides near the bullet hole and realized the tool must have been a protractor since it seemed to measure angles, too.

Deep-set green eyes looked over at her suddenly, as if he just remembered her presence.

"Feel free to call my department, Miss—?"

"Everhart." She stood, dropping the phone back into its cradle before returning his badge. "Tabitha Everhart."

He took the leather case from her hand, their fingers brushing briefly. The current of awareness surprised her since it was something she hadn't experienced in a very long time. Had he felt the jolt?

Yanking her hand back, she recalled her promise to herself when she first realized she needed to leave her ex. No more men for a while—sizzle or no sizzle.

"Warren Vitalis. I'm not on duty tonight. I just happened to be walking my dog when I heard a shot. Are you sure you're okay?"

"I'm fine. Just startled." She felt as though she'd been living on too much sugar and caffeine—all spun up but shaky and empty. "You said you were walking a dog?"

"Buster's outside. He's not a police dog so he didn't get to come in." The detective packed up his protractor and shifted his attention to the back of her sofa. He frowned at a dark mark in the middle of the worn fabric. A bullet hole. "Got a plastic bag or some household gloves?"

Tabitha could only stare at the bullet lodged in her couch. The bullet that had invaded her privacy, her life, her safety.

"Ms. Everhart?" His voice softened on the syllables of her name, making her eyes burn with the realization that she could be in serious danger.

"Yes." Grateful for a job that would pry her eyes away from the tiny bit of metal that could have been deadly, she raced into the kitchen before she lost control of her emotions. Ten seconds with her head under a faucet pouring cold water on her face and she'd be okay.

Please God, let her be okay.

It wasn't until a bit of lace around her thighs snagged on a shelf in the pantry as she leaned in for the sandwich-sized plastic bags that she remembered she'd been wearing a silky little nightgown around her apartment tonight. In an effort to ward off a dark mood she'd tried to pamper herself and feel beautiful, to soak her toes in a foot bath and luxuriate in her best silk nightie, instead of hanging out in a ten-year-old T-shirt and flannel pajamas with her hair in a ponytail.

No wonder Detective Vitalis had quickly busied himself with crime-scene investigation instead of asking her about what happened.

She'd been giving the man a free show he'd been too polite to point out.

WARREN THANKED JESUS, Mary and Joseph for the clothes Tabitha Everhart had decided to put on while she'd been retrieving a plastic bag and he'd called for backup. At least now, he could make eye contact with the sizzling redhead for more than two seconds. The inherent male need to check her out had eased since she'd ditched a mostly transparent swatch of lace and silk for the thorough coverage of flannel pajama bottoms and a bulky fisherman's sweater that hid a truly stellar set of curves.

If only his memory hadn't recalled the sight of her half-naked quite so well.

Petite and delicate-boned, she'd inherited the superfair skin that often goes with red hair, the bridge of her nose dusted with light freckles. Thin, arched eyebrows outlined wide brown eyes and her high cheekbones glowed a pink shade that hadn't been there before she left the room.

He sat across from her now on a battered wooden rocker draped with a pink silk scarf, making a few notes while she scratched Buster's head. He'd tried to tell her that Buster was a dog he'd rescued, a candidate for doggy death row because he'd bitten his former owner, even though Warren had never seen any evidence of viciousness. The dog was protective—sure. But what cop wouldn't appreciate a canine that didn't let anyone get the drop on him? And Buster had always liked women best anyway, the damn player. The animal lay with his head on Tabitha's thigh, giving Warren surreptitious looks of superiority out of one contented brown eye.

"You can't think of anyone who'd want to hurt you or even just harass you? Since the curtains aren't completely opaque, I have to think the shooter didn't aim to hit you. Did you realize how visible you are from the street?"

He didn't mean to censure her for her wardrobe choices, but damn. She needed heavier curtains if she was going to wander around in a street-level apartment dressed in that outfit she'd been wearing. Residual heat flared to life all over again at the memory.

"Oh. I guess not." Her hand stilled on the dog's head. "And no one I know would resort to such openly brutal actions. In my business, people tend to do more damage to one another at a social level. You know, slight someone at a party or start a rumor about an enemy."

He wondered if people like her had any idea how privileged they were to live in that kind of world, a far cry from the open cruelty Warren had witnessed his whole life.

"A patrol car will be here soon to go over the scene more thoroughly, but as long as I'm here we could get a few of the questions out of the way." When she didn't protest, he followed up on her last comment. "Where do you work?"

"I'm a body double." The answering lift of her chin was slight but noticeable.

He wondered why the job was cause to be defensive.

"Is there much call for that kind of work in New York?" He pictured that as a Hollywood profession, but he could certainly see this woman fulfilling that kind of role.

And thanks for the reminder of the high, full breasts and sweetly puckered nipples that he'd glimpsed beneath her negligee. He'd be lucky to get through this interview without breaking into a sweat.

"I keep busy enough. A lot of the soap operas are shot in New York and now that they allow more skin on daytime television, the actresses are put in more compromising positions than ever before. If they don't feel comfortable with a shower scene or a love scene, I stand in for the most brazen moments."

"Any resentment among your peers for how much work you get or jealousy from the women you stand in for?"

She looked down at Buster and cupped his ear as she stroked his fur. Was she thinking or stalling?

"My ex-husband had affairs with a few of the women on daytime TV, but I don't see why any of them would resent me these days. My husband and I parted ways nearly a year ago and the divorce has been final for months."

That sounded like a recipe for disaster. And what kind of scumbag landed a wife like this woman and then turned around and sabotaged it by screwing around behind her back?

Even Buster lifted his head long enough to look incensed.

"Was the divorce contentious?" He tried to maintain an open mind about the woman. She might be hot, but for all Warren knew she could be possessive or high maintenance. Women in film had a certain reputation, after all.

"He cheated on me with multiple women, Detective. It was definitely difficult." Her lips pursed tight. Held.

"But you don't think he'd want to hurt you?"

"Not with violence."

"Ms. Everhart, I'm going to be honest with you and say I think there's a decent chance your window was pierced by stray gunfire from a dispute that didn't involve you. But you can't be too careful when there was only one bullet fired in a neighborhood that doesn't see a lot of random criminal mischief." He asked her for the names of the women her husband slept with as well as the ex himself before scribbling them down on a pilfered piece of paper from a stray notebook on her overloaded coffee table. "So let the police help you decide who might be violent and who isn't before you withhold information about a recent divorce. Are you sure there's no one else in your life that might want to make trouble for you?"

"No one that I'm aware of." She clutched a bright yellow satin throw pillow to her chest, the movement jerky. Uneasy.

"Are you sure you'll be all right alone tonight?" He

hated it that this had happened on his block, the same route he jogged every night and considered his backyard. "You definitely don't want to stay in your apartment with the window compromised and the lock broken on your door."

He regretted the need to bust in here, but she could have been hurt…or worse.

Tonight's incident with Tabitha hadn't exactly mirrored the hellish night of his sixteenth birthday, but the scream and the gunshot had freaked him out for a few minutes, had him busting into her apartment like a SWAT guy. But the mental trip down memory lane never failed to bring out his inner vigilante—the need to protect that went beyond his badge.

"I'll be fine. I'm sure the shot wasn't meant for my window and I'll call tomorrow to have the glass replaced."

"But you won't try to stay here." He didn't want her anywhere near the apartment until they'd had the chance to go over everything in detail.

He'd seen the shell casing embedded in the back of her couch earlier and he'd toyed with the idea of removing it but it had been lodged tightly in a hardwood interior and he didn't want to compromise the scene without the proper tools. Besides, seeing a bullet pried out of their possessions tended to freak some people out and he hadn't had enough time to accomplish the task while she'd been out of the room. As a longtime ballistics expert, Warren already knew the shell belonged to a .38, a weapon that wasn't exactly the firearm of choice of today's bigger-is-better street thugs.

"I can stay at a hotel tonight. I'll be okay."

Something about her tone made him think she was trying hard to convince herself more than him. But then, Warren would bet his badge this woman was an expert in talking herself through hardship. Her whole apartment spoke of hard times covered over with brightly decorated facades, optimism in the face of anguish. He had to admire that kind of grit.

"Fine. There's just one more thing. I'll run a few tests on the bullet just to see if anything unusual comes up, but is there any chance you know anyone who carries a .38?"

She stilled. Buster nudged his snout back under her hand to restart her attentions.

"Ms. Everhart?"

"Call me Tabitha." She scratched the dog idly but didn't meet Warren's gaze. "I don't know any sane person who would carry a gun around the streets of New York, Detective."

That answer begged a follow-up question, but she stood abruptly and strode toward the kitchen, her bare feet falling with the smallest of sounds on the hardwood floors covered with thin throw rugs.

"Can I get you some water? You said you were out running." She came back with a bottle for him and then hastened to the sink to fill a bowl for Buster. "You both must be thirsty."

When she had run out of activity and stood awkwardly beside her dining room table some twelve feet away from him, Warren asked the question she so obviously didn't want to answer. The lights of an approaching squad car reflected blue and red through the window, broadcasting the arrival of his backup.

"Who owns a .38, Tabitha?"

She paused for a long moment, then cocked a hip against a lopsided table propped up by a stack of books on one end, the movement of her body a subtle reminder of the famous curves that hid beneath the big sweater.

"Honestly, Detective? *I* do."

2

TABITHA SAT ON the fire escape outside her on-location shoot the next afternoon and tilted her face up toward the sun's rays. Wrapped in her winter coat over a bathrobe, she waited for her call to the set and tried to swallow down the attack of nerves that always came with her body double work.

"We'll be ready for you in just a minute, Tabitha," one of the set assistants called out the door where she sat in a cast-iron patio chair chilled from months of a New York winter.

"Thanks." She smiled weakly, her game face not quite assembled yet after last night's stray bullet scare and a sexy cop diving headfirst through the front door.

Oddly, she half wondered which event had rattled her more. The bullet had been scary, no doubt. But the man…wow. After her divorce, warm feelings for men in general had sort of disappeared. And there was a certain comfort in that lack of emotion after life kicked your butt. Last night had been a wake-up call to her snoozing hormones, however. Warren Vitalis ignited some serious heat with just one look.

In the distance she heard a police siren. Would she ever see the hot detective again? Or had he handed over her case to the patrol cops who had shown up later in the evening after she'd admitted the only person she knew with a .38 was *her?* Detective Vitalis's suggestion that her ex could have been involved in the shooting last night was ludicrous since her former husband had always been far too concerned with appearances and what other people thought of him to lower himself to gangster tactics.

No, Manny Redding had too many other more subtle weapons to hurt her. The cheating creep.

"We're ready now, Tabitha," the set assistant called out, ending any time for psyching herself up for this scene.

Damn it.

Today wasn't just a run-of-the-mill soap opera shower scene. Tabitha had been a little nervous about this gig—a prime-time movie special for a cable network—from the moment she'd learned she would be standing in for the actress playing a prostitute. Worse, the prostitute was in her late teens and Tabitha's body was clearly that of a woman on the far side of twenty-five. She'd be thirty next year. Could she still pass off her bod as a nineteen-year-old's?

Planting one foot in front of the other, she congratulated herself that at least she hadn't resorted to any of the unhealthy eating tactics she'd struggled with in the past. She'd worked her tail off for the lean muscle tone she had these days. One of the best benefits of her spectacularly messy divorce was the clear head that allowed her to be healthy again. She'd silenced her ex-husband's voice in her head telling her she wasn't cut out to be on film. That she shouldn't share her talents with the world when he needed her working behind the scenes for him.

And finally, that no other man should look at *his* wife.

The subtle possessiveness that started off as sort of endearing eventually became suffocating and for a few dark months toward the end she'd staved off the anxiety with food. The bulimia she'd struggled with as a teen resurfaced with a vengeance.

She was under control again now. Every day that she bared her body for the camera now soothed a little more of her wounded ego and healed the part of her that knew she'd stayed in a bad marriage for too long. Besides, body double work was just a means to an end to finance her return to filmmaking.

Allowing her coat to slide off her shoulders, she didn't bother counting the number of people on the closed set the way she used to when she first started life as a body double. By now, she didn't care how many people saw her mostly naked because she was stronger. More fearless.

And screw them if they couldn't appreciate an almost thirty-year-old's body forged of sweat and discipline.

Letting the bathrobe slip from her shoulders, she allowed the world to see her flesh-toned body stocking that covered only the most crucial parts. The custom-made nude thong matched her skin color exactly. The pasties she wore on her nipples weren't half as cute as the one Janet Jackson had once famously displayed to the world, but Tabitha's more functional brand made sure her nipples didn't show up unexpectedly in any camera shots.

There were no costume malfunctions when Tabitha was in charge.

Tabitha walked toward the bed where the scene called for her to fake a sexual encounter with the aging former Hollywood bad boy who'd been relegated to made-for-TV movies after hitting rehab too many times. He was handsome enough, she supposed, if you liked a guy in makeup with a sock covering his privates.

But as Tabitha strode toward the bed, her mind suddenly replaced the actor with a vision of Detective Warren Vitalis lying between those sheets waiting for her, his virile male body taking up much more of the bed than her current co-star.

A wave of want halted her in her tracks and sent pleasurable shivers over her bare skin.

Ooh.

There couldn't have been a more supremely bad time for her mind to play tricks on her or for her hibernating libido to come roaring back to life. Her cheeks flushed, not from embarrassment so much as that preorgasmic full body tingle she'd only vaguely remembered until this moment. Her nipples tightened beneath their cover-ups and she half feared the self-adhesive pasties would pop right off her suddenly excited body.

Scavenging every bit of willpower she possessed, she forced herself to see the makeup line on her co-star's neck, to remember where she was and that she wanted to get this scene over with. The sexy detective might have her fantasizing, but she couldn't allow wishful thinking to cloud her vision ever again.

Lust had landed her in the worst sort of marriage. She'd be damned if something so insubstantial as sexual attraction would ever steer her into the arms of any man who didn't see beyond the surface to appreciate the woman inside.

WARREN STALKED THROUGH the old building a block behind Central Park West in search of the camera crew. In search of one woman in particular. Tabitha's casting agent had given Warren a hell of a runaround this morning, but once he'd finally pried an address out of the guy, Warren had hightailed it to the shoot to have another crack at the closemouthed body double.

She hadn't been totally honest with him the night before and that pissed him off. She'd admitted to owning a .38 that had been a gift from her husband while they'd been married. What she hadn't bothered sharing was the fact that it had been reported stolen long before her divorce was finalized.

She also hadn't bothered sharing the fact that her divorce had been acrimonious and high-profile since her ex was a powerful New York producer. Why would she want to protect a guy who—judging by the claims volleyed at her in the tabloids—had been determined to drag her name through the mud during divorce proceedings?

The questions gnawed away at him after he'd gone

to the station to file an incident report and do a little homework. Tabitha's vacant eyes when he'd first entered her apartment had eaten at his conscience, telling him she'd probably been in shock when he dove into her apartment and pointed a gun at her.

"Detective Vitalis, NYPD." He announced himself at the door once he found the right apartment and then flashed his badge a few more times to gain access to the room where Tabitha was shooting.

Several crewmembers tried to explain the concept of "closed set" to him on his way in, but he'd always been good with people and adept at using the authority of his position to get where he needed to be. He didn't want to stop the shoot, but he had to admit a definite interest in seeing Tabitha Everhart at work.

And when was the last time he'd felt that kind of intense interest in any woman? Occasional nights with holster groupies had never engendered the kind of heat Tabitha had with nothing beyond her presence.

Slipping silently into the huge master suite where her scene was being shot, however, he began to realize maybe he didn't need to see *this*. The room was darkened but crowded with camera people and crewmembers despite the "closed" label. At the center of the silent movement on the fringes of the room, Tabitha Everhart sat on top of a smug-looking bastard in a bed of rumpled white sheets and fat pillows. The two of them were highlighted by umbrella lights and spotlights with diffusers stretched over the lamps. The perfect lighting illuminated every square inch of Tabitha's barely covered skin.

Warren had thought for one heart-stopping instant that she was buck naked on top of the guy, but soon he'd spotted the tiny cups that hugged her nipples and the hint of flesh-toned strap around her hip that gave away she must be wearing panties.

Her deep red hair was pinned up, possibly to make sure it was kept out of the shot. The director seemed fixated on filming the actor's hands on Tabitha's back, judging by the monitors stationed near his camera. The shoot seemed focused on body parts instead of facial expressions. That made sense given Tabitha's job, but it was disconcerting as hell to watch lovemaking broken down into a step-by-step pantomime that seemed cold and calculated, stilted and awkward.

Once the fascination with the strange process wore off, Warren could focus on details besides the fact that Tabitha was mostly naked. He studied her expression and found her miles away from her job as if she consciously disconnected from the work. It bothered him to realize he liked that idea because her co-star looked totally into the moment, the guy's superior "I'm the stud of the free world" expression really getting on Warren's nerves.

But Tabitha was clearly distracted, her body moving automatically when the director called for her to slide her hand up her own thigh or—worse—slide her hand up the actor's thigh.

How had she learned to disassociate herself from those touches, the practiced intimacy of the camera shots? Was it simply the mark of a professional body double to perform her duties with such clear distance? Or had Tabitha Everhart learned to remove herself from her work for personal reasons? Maybe she was unhappy with the job. Bored. Did she take it for granted that she was a beautiful woman whose curves were so perfect that other women clamored for her to stand in their place?

The thought bugged him almost as much as the fact that she'd lied to him through omission the night before. After growing up in a violent household based on keeping up appearances, Warren didn't appreciate people who hid dangerous secrets. It wouldn't matter how many thieves, dealers or murderers Warren kept off the streets through his job. He'd never bring his father back. He'd never fix the fact that he'd kept his family's secrets until all their lives imploded.

"That's a good take," the director shouted, interrupting the dark directions of Warren's thoughts. "Let's get Maureen back in here," the director continued, releasing Tabitha from her close clinch with the actor who held her a second too long after the shot was finished.

Was there something going on between her and the actor? Warren realized he didn't like that idea at all. Not that he had any designs on the hot divorcée, especially if a deceptive personality went along with those killer curves.

But Warren recognized her cohort actor as a former big-league star who'd been a notorious womanizer and drug user.

The guy smiled wolfishly at Tabitha's back view as she walked away from the set toward the door to the makeup room behind where Warren stood. She didn't see him for a moment, her eyes blinking against the change in light, and Warren did all he could to keep his jaw off the ground at the sight of her. Heat rushed south along with his blood and his sense.

She had the kind of body men went stupid over. Lush, high breasts that swayed just enough when she walked to advertise the wares were 100 percent authentic gifts from God and not a surgeon. He'd only just begun to take the scenic journey to her hips when an assistant hurried over to give her a long white bathrobe to wrap herself in. A good thing since it was time for Warren to go to work.

He cleared his throat and breathed in a steadying gulp of air. Too bad her scent filtered through, seducing his senses with the knowledge of how she smelled.

Clean. Like soap rather than fragrance. The intimate realization made him want to know what her hair smelled like, too. *Hell.*

"Tabitha, may I speak to you a moment if you're done with your day?"

He already knew she was finished since one of the assistants had told him the bed scene was her only responsibility to the production today. But after she'd given him half answers the night before, he was curious to see how far she would go to avoid speaking to him again.

"Detective." Her hand flew to the collar of her robe, where she clutched the neckline just long enough to be sure it was closed. An odd response from a woman who'd just walked around a bedroom mostly naked in front of at least ten other people. Did he make her uncomfortable? Or was she as aware of the heat between them as him?

"Do you have a minute?" he pressed, struggling to keep his thoughts on the investigation. He was ready for some answers about her gun, the shot through her window and a marriage that had gone down in flames in a very public fashion.

"Of course." She tugged at the clip in her hair and brought the whole red mass falling down around her shoulders in unruly disarray. "Just give me a minute to change and I'll meet you by the front door."

Nodding, Warren headed to the living area of the spacious apartment that someone had given over to the day's shoot. He settled in on a sofa to wait for Tabitha and tried not to imagine her peeling off those tiny pasties in a room down the hall.

WHEN SHE CAUGHT HERSELF swiping a brush through her hair for at least the fiftieth time, Tabitha realized she couldn't stall any longer on the inevitable talk with Detective Vitalis.

She'd changed into a long khaki skirt and a yellow tank with a sweater over it, but she couldn't quite shake the feeling of nakedness around him since he'd first seen her in a skimpy nightgown and now he'd watched her work, for heaven knew how long, in little more than a thong. Surely if she made it through today's interview with her head held high she could call her old insecurities dead and gone.

And there was a chance she could have done it if only

she had a few more layers of clothes. A burka maybe. Or a poncho at the very least. Her attraction to the man made her feel far more naked and aware of herself than her body double gig.

Tucking her brush back in her work bag, she said goodbye to the stylist and the makeup person before venturing out into the ultramodern living room furnished with white plastic cubes for tables and white sectional pieces that could be moved all around the room for optimal seating. Manny had hired a decorator to do their house in all white once, a decorating palette as cold and unforgiving as their marriage had eventually become.

Tabitha's apartment as a single woman looked like a living patchwork quilt with colors thrown everywhere as vivid reminders she'd survived the isolating hell of marriage Siberia.

The detective stood as she entered the room that suddenly reminded her of a padded cell for crazy people. And while Tabitha appreciated the well-bred manners of a man who stood when a woman came in the room, she needed to be out of this apartment without delay.

"Hi, Detective. Sorry it took me so long, but I wondered if we could move our conversation to somewhere more private and less…white?" She didn't know how else to say it, but getting away from the inside of this icebox room was high on her list of immediate priorities.

Being shot at made a woman feel vulnerable enough without having the added complications of knee-weakening attraction and memories of a bad marriage to go with it. The attraction she couldn't help. But the surroundings had to go.

"No problem." He didn't hesitate, only moved toward the door to open it for her. "Where would you like to go?"

"There's a coffee shop a few blocks down. I got a latte there on my way in this morning." She could breathe again once they left the apartment behind them.

"Not exactly more private, is it?" They took the stairs down two flights since the old-fashioned building had a beautiful staircase central to the residence, instead of the emergency stairwells built on new structures like an afterthought.

"Actually, it was really quiet earlier, but if you have another idea?" She adjusted the strap of her work tote on her shoulder as they left the building and strode out onto the street into mild afternoon pedestrian traffic. The neighborhood was more residential than commercial, with elegant facades and a wealth of domestic help walking dogs, parking cars and carrying groceries into the buildings where they worked.

"No. That's fine. But what have you got against white?"

"It's a long story I refuse to bore anyone with. Not even a detective intent on asking me questions." Her mood lifted out on the street, her comfort level higher hanging out with dog walkers and personal shoppers than the high-powered people who could afford those luxuries.

"I wouldn't be here today, Tabitha, if you'd been honest with me last night."

That halted her in her tracks.

"I was very honest with you." She'd admitted she

owned a gun—a weapon forced on her by Manny as a Christmas gift one year.

She pointed out the coffee shop as they cleared the next street, her apprehension returning as quickly as it had fled. Her state of agitation wasn't helped by the fact that Warren's strong arm reached around behind her to open the door, his torso coming in momentary contact with her back. Awareness skittered down her spine to pool at the base and tingle through her hips.

"You neglected to mention you and your ex were at one another's throats during your divorce when I asked about enemies."

Just when Tabitha had caught her breath from feeling his chest close to her back, he lay one palm lightly on her spine to steer her toward a table in the far corner of the shop. The place was decorated with Italian marble and granite tabletops, but Tabitha would venture into the most upscale of businesses if there was good coffee to be had. The colors were yellow-gold and brown with a few muted blues mixed in the Venetian artwork. Best of all, there were several empty tables spaced far apart.

Tabitha waited until Warren's hand disappeared from her spine and they were seated safely across from one another to respond.

"I didn't mean to suggest my ex-husband and I like one another, Detective. I just wanted to make it clear that my ex wouldn't purposely try to hurt me. Physically." He'd sure as hell put her through the wringer other ways, but violence? Not his style.

"Are you sure about that?" He held up a hand to the

waitress who approached and the woman backed off to give them more time.

"Yes." She didn't appreciate his tone that implied she would lie. "Look, if Manny Redding wanted to hurt me he would have done so when I broke up his Valentine's Day rendezvous with an up-and-coming actress. He'd been angry enough then at my public meltdown in the foyer of a friend's house party where Manny had been banging his starlet in a downstairs bathroom."

"Ah, hell." He scrubbed a hand through his shorn hair, not moving the bristly strands one bit. "I know the questions must suck, but—"

She interrupted, unable to tamp down the old fury that still surprised her sometimes.

"You have no idea. But if Manny wanted to hurt me physically, I guarantee he would have done it right then. If you have evidence to the contrary, by all means, please share it."

"Fair enough." The detective leaned forward over the table to reach for her hand. He glided his fingers over the back of hers for a moment before he seemed to catch himself. He backed off slowly.

The gesture caught her off guard coming from the man who'd pointed a gun at her the night before and who seemed to think she'd deliberately withheld information. Still, the misplaced nature of the touch didn't make it any less potent. The heat he'd started inside her last night simmered again, reminding her it wasn't going away anytime soon.

"Tabitha, when you told me last night that you

owned a .38, you didn't say anything about the gun being missing."

Blinking, she tried to ignore the hedonistic wants of her body to make sense of his words.

"It's not missing." Confused, she waited for him to explain what the hell he meant by that. "I keep it in a gun case in my closet. The same place since I first moved in to the apartment."

"Have you *opened* the gun case lately?"

A sick feeling bubbled in her stomach and not even the scent of coffee couldn't take away the impending nausea.

"I—I've always hated the sight of that thing."

"Your ex reported the weapon stolen from the home you shared over a year ago."

3

HE NEEDED TO BACK the hell off.

Warren scrolled through old newspaper archives on his home computer the next afternoon and told himself he shouldn't be spending his day off digging through Tabitha's past after the flood of inappropriate thoughts he'd been having about her from their first very unorthodox meeting. But then, if he was being honest with himself, hadn't he taken the day off from work *purposely* to see what he could find out about this ex of hers?

"Producer's Partying Puts Wife Over the Edge" read one headline on his most recent search, making Warren incensed that tabloid journalists could soft sell infidelity as *partying*.

Technically, a stray shot through a woman's window was not an official NYPD investigation yet. He'd filed a report in case she had any more trouble, but without any concrete reason to suspect she'd been targeted, the work Warren did this afternoon was strictly out of personal interest.

Personal because—hell, he couldn't deny it—he was attracted to Tabitha. When they'd parted ways at the coffee shop the day before, he'd had to hold his tongue firmly beneath his teeth to keep from suggesting he escort her home and be there at her side when she looked to see if her gun was in its case. He *wanted* to be there for her because he knew what she would find—a gut hunch confirmed by her phone call an hour after he'd gotten back to the precinct. There was no gun in the case, just a pile of bullets nestled in the foam cutout of the gun to weigh down the pouch.

"Aspiring Actress Loses Prime Part Amid Blackball Accusations." The next headline that caught his eye was taken from a more reliable source than the article about Tabitha going "over the edge" about her ex's partying.

Apparently Tabitha had wanted to be a character actress at one point—a more prominent role in the community where she now worked as a silent participant. According to the story, she'd lost a recurring role on a popular soap opera after she'd filed for divorce, and she'd publicly accused Manny of pulling the strings to make it happen. Bastard.

The more stories that Warren scrolled through, the more pissed off he became at a guy who would try to railroad his wife's career simply because she didn't let him get away with flagrant adultery. Warren couldn't help but relate to the woman whose life had been steered off course by someone hell bent on revenge. But it wasn't until he discovered an old photo of Tabitha in a decorating magazine ensconced on a pristine white couch in the middle of a snow-white living room that he knew he couldn't back off Tabitha Everhart.

She sat alone and off center in the photo of a palatial living room, a vibrant woman with flaming hair and a heart-stopping smile. A woman with dreams she'd been forced to reroute because she'd gotten involved with a man who thought what she wanted didn't matter.

Shutting down his computer, he whistled to Buster and decided to take his run early today—right past Tabitha's place. There was no law against what he was thinking about doing, no code of ethics that prevented him from seeing her again on a personal level since there hadn't been an official investigation into the incident at her place.

He had no idea what he was going to say to her, but then, if things went his way, maybe they wouldn't be talking at all.

MAYBE THE GUN really *had* been stolen.

Tabitha stared at the empty case on the middle of her coffee table and tried to remember those last few days in her old house before she'd moved out. Manny had hardly spoken to her. His fury at the scene she'd made had embarrassed him, putting an impenetrable wall between the two of them. So maybe he'd just been too angry to let her know there'd been a break-in, too caught up in his silent grudge to speak to her about anything, but he'd done the right thing and phoned in the missing weapon to the police.

She hoped that's what happened.

Still, the incident didn't add up.

Day had turned to evening while she ventured back

in time in her mind. The blanket she'd stapled over her newly replaced front window wasn't attractive, but it provided a thicker barrier than her curtains until she could afford massive drapes that made her feel less on display.

She revealed enough of herself at work without having her whole life visible through her front window. There was only one man she might like to reveal a little more of herself to, and she knew that had the potential to be a big mistake. Besides, Detective Vitalis had seemed mistrustful of her the last time they met. What good could come from an attraction tempered by suspicion?

So it came as a surprise when she heard a bark outside her front door a few moments later, followed by a quick, efficient knock.

"Tabitha?"

Warren's deep masculine tone penetrated the repaired door easily. And God help her but how did she end up thinking about Warren and *penetrated* in the same moment?

Her subconscious was working overtime.

She had the vague sense of being caught doing something naughty since she'd just been thinking about what she'd like to do with him if he wasn't a cop poking through the skeletons in her closet. He seemed safer to fantasize about when he wasn't close enough for her to actually act on those thoughts.

Confirming that it was indeed Warren who stood on the concrete steps out front, she unfastened the bolt and opened the door.

"Glad to see you're using the dead bolt now." He smiled crookedly while Buster dispensed with the formalities and attempted to push his way past her.

She noticed Warren looked over the repairs to the doorframe as he stood on her threshold.

"I figured I didn't want any more strangers bursting in here with a gun drawn. Come on in." She stood aside to let both man and dog inside, gesturing toward her assembly of mismatched furniture that was cast in a reddish glow, thanks to a sheer scarf thrown over a table lamp by the window.

Buster hurried right over to the bowl of water she'd left out since his last visit, a sad testament to her cleaning ethic. While the dog slurped briefly and then sniffed his way around her apartment, she closed the door behind them.

"Have a seat." Her apartment seemed smaller with Warren in it, his presence making her very aware of how much she'd avoided men for the past year.

Maybe she was only attracted to him because she'd been severely orgasm-deprived? Yeah, right. Whatever the man did to keep fit was sure as hell working. He was all lean muscle.

"Tabitha." He didn't sit when she did.

"What? Is this about the gun? Did you find out anything?" She rose again, more nervous because of her inappropriate thoughts than because of the conversation about a deadly weapon. How strange was that?

"Not yet." He came closer now, lowering himself onto the couch as if to make her sit back down, too. "I just wanted to make it clear to you before we got too comfortable that I'm not here on business."

Oh. Her pulse jumped in response, immediately interested in this new development.

"You're not?" She dropped back on those couch cushions with no conscious thought, landing too close to the attractive detective who wasn't paying her a business call.

Oh my.

"No. This is strictly a social call, so feel free to boot us out if you're busy." He looked around for Buster, who was already walking in circles near the fireplace as if trying to find that perfect place to sleep.

Would the detective be as quick to make himself comfortable here? Her mouth watered.

"I'm not busy." The words rushed out of her mouth so fast she probably sounded like exactly what she was—an undersexed divorcée too long deprived.

Why did men have to continue to tempt her after all she'd been through thanks to the penis-bearing half of the species? Damn biology.

"It occurred to me tonight that since there is no official investigation into the bullet through your window—just an incident on file—there was nothing stopping me from asking you to…dinner sometime."

The way he paused over the invitation made her question what else he had on his mind besides dinner.

Especially since he looked at her for the first time in the man-to-woman way instead of the cop-to-victim way. His eyes lingered, so warm and inviting on her that she had to glance down at herself to be sure she hadn't accidentally greeted him in her nightie again. But nope. She was respectably dressed in a calf-length plaid skirt and a short white cardigan sweater. Very Park Avenue despite her downtown address.

So it wasn't her outfit causing any kind of sensation here. Heat unfurled between her hips. She needed to stop this before she did something she regretted.

Like tackle him to the floor and tear his clothes off. It would be fine for a one-night stand, but what if the gunshot incident turned into something more dangerous down the road? She'd hate to compromise her relationship with a man who made her feel far more safe and protected than any of the patrol officers who'd followed up on the call that night.

"Dinner? I hate to be blunt, Detective—"

"Call me Warren."

"Warren." She tasted the name on her lips and liked it a little too well.

"And please be blunt. I'm not a man who appreciates false facades."

The wealth of possible meaning beneath that statement intrigued her. Who had shown Warren a false facade in the past?

"Okay. Warren." She couldn't resist the warmth of that name, the intimacy of calling him by it one more time. "Then I'll be honest with you. I'm not in a good place to consider dinner dates or any kind of normal dating scenario."

"So that's a no?" He shifted on the couch, angling slightly closer by turning to face her.

The diamond in his ear caught her eye, making her wonder about the show of sparkle on an otherwise Spartan-looking man. The earring fascinated her, as did the rest of him. Her ex had been all about the dazzle—he probably had more carats than that in the insignia on his money clip, let alone the collection of rings he'd taken to sporting after he'd sealed a deal with a silent partner that moved him into a much higher earning bracket.

And his hair—Manny would have never had the balls to come as close to shaving his head as Warren had. She reached to touch the bristly hair at his temple and caught herself. Stopped herself.

What was she thinking?

"I'm not in a good place in my life for any kind of relationship." And wasn't that the God's honest truth? As much as she'd love to indulge a few fantasies with this man, she wasn't putting herself in a position to get her heart stomped again. Or her pride. Or any other part of her, damn it.

"So you're not interested in a relationship. Who says this has to be more than just dinner?" His arm unfolded across the back of the couch until she could feel the heat of his skin close to her shoulders, his hand coming to rest lightly on the back of her head, fingers sifting gently through the ends of her hair until her scalp tingled pleasantly.

And that wasn't the only tingle.

Her eyelids grew heavy at the hypnotic brush of his

fingers through her hair, the solid male presence of him beside her urging her to lean on him, into him, all over him.

Oh, that sounded unwise. And tempting.

"Since when is dinner ever just dinner? I've been alone too long to sit through polite small talk." Since her marriage had fallen apart, she'd given up couching her words in social niceties.

"You think you'll be bored?" Warren was clearly on another wavelength since that wasn't at all what she'd been thinking.

She couldn't help the short bark of laughter that escaped her lips.

"Not likely." Her gaze locked with his and she felt herself being pulled closer. Willed closer. But she didn't know who was doing the willing.

"Then what does being alone have to do with you not being able to make it through dinner?" That soft scrub of his fingers shifted from her hair to the back of her neck.

"Besides sending the wrong message about my dating availability?" Maybe she should have taken him up on dinner. "I'm way too impatient to sit through chitchat when all I want—"

She still couldn't quite put it into words. She trailed off as his fingers sought a path down the curve of her neck to her shoulder. The cardigan sweater that had seemed respectable enough when she answered the door now gave him access to bare skin since she'd left the top button undone.

If she wasn't careful, *she'd* be coming undone next.

"What do you want?" he prompted, steering her

gently back to the conversation they'd been having, the one in which she'd almost admitted to dark desires for a downtown detective.

Her heart pounded so loudly she couldn't hear herself think through the noise. No. *Admit it, Tabitha.* She just wasn't thinking at all.

"I don't know about you. But I really only want dessert." The sordid truth of the matter sat between them for only a moment before her confession ignited something explosive.

She arched up to him, drawn to him and unwilling to pretend she wasn't. She wanted this man. Badly.

Lips parting, she kissed him. Sensation rippled through her chest, fluttering down to her belly and tingling outward.

For long moments, she simply breathed his air, her mouth hovering lightly against his. He didn't press her, didn't touch her anywhere except that feather-light caress of his hand on her shoulder.

He tasted like peppermint. The scent mixed with the vanilla lip gloss she'd put on at some point that day. Courage growing along with the liquid warmth threatening to swallow her, Tabitha couldn't wait any longer to test the texture of the rest of his mouth. Her tongue came in brief, hot contact with his lips, darting along the fullness of the middle before she wound her arms around his neck and pressed her whole body against him.

He surprised her by breaking the contact, pulling back when she'd been debating another move forward.

Had he realized she'd been about to tackle him? The twinge of disappointment startled her as much as the way her heart jumped in nervous rhythm.

"You're agreeing to dessert then, right?" He relinquished her shoulder to smooth his way up her neck and cup her chin. "I want to make sure we understand each other before we go any further."

"You want clarification?" Her fingers reached up to touch the open collar of his shirt and she remembered how he mentioned not liking people with false facades. Lucky for him, she was all too glad to be honest about this. "I'm interested in exploring this attraction wherever it leads, but I'm not going down the path of dinner or drinks or a standing Friday-night commitment for all the orgasms in the world."

"I'll make sure not to bother you on Fridays." A hint of a smile twitched his lips before he ventured near again, but now that Tabitha had found her voice, she couldn't seem to silence it. She had to share one more, very important thing.

"But if we're going to follow this where it leads, could you do me one small favor?" She pressed her hand to his chest at the last minute and got to experience the solid warmth of him.

Her hand splayed against his heart.

"Name it." His heart hammered quickly beneath her hand in a way that fascinated her. Flattered her even more.

"Just be careful you don't touch any more than my lips until we're ready to take this to its natural conclusion." She'd always had intimacy problems. Bad timing with her...er, climaxes. "I'm sort of a sexual powder keg after too many nights alone and—" deep, steadying breath "—I think I have a pretty sensitive trigger by now."

4

A STUNNINGLY BEAUTIFUL WOMAN who was a self-proclaimed sexual powder keg wanted a no-strings relationship with him?

Warren had to check his horoscope to see if all kinds of planets were aligned because this kind of thing did *not* happen to him. His world was a brutal place, not some red-hot fairy tale with a curvy siren in a starring role.

He studied Tabitha in the crimson glow of the lamp. Was it just the light that suffused her cheeks with color as he leaned closer to align their bodies without touching?

Her eyelids fluttered once, twice, then closed as she tilted her chin to meet his mouth. The need to feel her skin, to hold her steady while he kissed her, rode him hard. He remembered the silky warmth of her when he'd stroked up her neck earlier, and he wanted to indulge the feel of her again. But a good man follows a woman's rules, right? Even while he did his damnedest to ensure *she* wouldn't want to follow them for long.

He just needed to make her touch *him,* and then all bets were off for the kind of restraint he needed to show today. Lips grazing hers, he sampled the vanilla-tinged flavor of her mouth more deeply, lingering in the places that made her squirm in her seat.

A blessedly easy task.

She sighed in the back of her throat, her hips tilting ever so slightly closer. He could tell because her body radiated heat as surely as she radiated sex appeal and every millimeter closer she got spiked the temperature in the room.

He really shouldn't take this too far tonight since their conversation had been tinged with the attraction they'd both been feeling. Didn't he owe her a sort of cooling-off period to make sure this was what she wanted? Not that he could necessarily walk away from her anyhow, but his sense of fair play suggested he should. But next time…he'd take her up on that dessert offer, by God. His blood was slamming through his arteries with excessive force. He couldn't tell if he was burning from the inside out or the outside in anymore. His swim training didn't do half the number on him that her kisses could.

Just when he figured he'd have to call uncle and admit defeat, Tabitha busted the "no touch" rule in spectacular fashion by wrapping her arms around him and drawing him down on top of her. Her breasts were suddenly pressed against his chest, the soft swells straining the buttons on her sweater as much as they strained his crumbling reserve. They'd been sitting on the couch, but now they listed to one side in an effort to connect as many square inches of their bodies as possible.

It had been too long for him. He'd hardly dated since

a divorce that was a hell of a lot older than hers. Three years. A few women. None of them like Tabitha.

She guided his hand to her cashmere-covered breast and that cooling-off period started to sound like a load of crap. She wanted him as badly as he wanted her, and that blew his mind. Her full breasts pressed against her clothes and toward his touch. Everything about her was soft and warm and he needed to lose himself inside her, surround himself with that kind of warmth. He popped two buttons free on her sweater before diving beneath the fabric for a handful of fragrant feminine flesh.

And she was fragrant. He'd been curious about the scent of her since he'd caught the hint of clean soapiness about her skin on the set. But the hollow between her breasts held another kind of perfume, sweetly exotic and all the more intoxicating because the knowledge seemed secret somehow. He breathed deep, losing his mind to anything but sexual thoughts.

Sprawling on top of her on the couch, he left one leg dragging on the floor, his hips in tight proximity to hers as his hands molded to the shape of her breasts through the feather-thin fabric of her bra. Her fingers raked through his hair and trailed down his back, scoring his shoulders right through the fabric of his shirt. He used his knee to find leverage between her legs, spreading her open to the touches he'd been holding back.

He abandoned her breast to reach under her skirt, stroking up one silken leg. If she had a sensitive trigger, how fair was it to make her wait? The justification made perfect sense and gave him permission to do everything he wanted to do with this woman.

Her taut calf gave way to her knee and the delicate place behind it that made her convulse just a little when he circled the soft skin. Leaving that tender spot for her thigh, he spread his hand wide to cover as much of her skin as possible, savoring the way her flesh felt hotter the nearer he came to the juncture of her legs.

His cell phone blared into his consciousness, shattering the hottest foreplay of his life with some obnoxious mechanical-sounding ring tone one of the guys at the precinct must have programmed for him.

"Damn it." He said worse things in his mind, but he didn't want to scare off Tabitha, who looked fairly dazed.

If he could dispatch this call in thirty seconds or less, maybe they could pick right up where they left off.

He reached into his jacket pocket on the second ring and hit the button to answer the call that he could see emanated from the precinct.

Not a good sign for handling this in a hurry.

"Vitalis here."

He tried to blink through the raw lust for Tabitha enough to concentrate on the phone call from another detective—a woman new to the detective squad who'd made her first big arrest last month. Donata Casale had raised a lot of eyebrows in the department when she came on board since she'd been a gangster's girlfriend at one time, but she'd clawed her way through police ranks with hardcore determination to change her life.

Warren respected the hell out of her, even if he didn't appreciate this particular interruption.

"Got a bullet embedded in brick. The guys say they can take it out with little peripheral damage, but I wanted to check with you first to see what you thought. I've got a homicide in the VIP room of a club downtown and the embedded bullet is at an odd angle. The victim is apparently a well-known porn star, John de Milo."

Warren knew Donata's partner—a seasoned vet—was out of town this week. Detectives with more experience might be apt to just remove the bullet and let Warren work through the ballistics issues in the office, but he could see the benefit to observing the bullet in play if the angle was a concern. A good extraction could be key in a case that had a lot riding on identifying a weapon. Any schmo could figure out what caliber a bullet was, but Warren's specialty was for matching particular bullets or shell casings with those at other scenes, or even tying them to evidence in cold cases. Knowing that the same firearm had discharged bullets in separate incidents had been critical evidence in plenty of investigations during his tenure with the NYPD.

Besides, Warren had personal reasons for making ballistics his life and they applied whether or not he was on the verge of the best sex of his life.

Not that he didn't regret it.

"Would you rather I just have the guys remove the bullet?" Donata asked, tipping him off that he'd been thinking too long.

And wishing he didn't have to walk out of Tabitha's apartment tonight.

"No. I can be downtown in fifteen minutes. What's the address?" He wrote the street number on a corner of newspaper on the coffee table and disconnected the call, only to realize Tabitha was already inching her way out from underneath him.

He regretted the need to leave her when she looked so deliciously disheveled with her bra strap falling off one shoulder and her sweater half undone. His heart still slammed hard, his body not quite getting the message that he wouldn't be able to have dessert tonight.

"Sorry." He straightened, pulling her up to a sitting position on the couch beside him. "I wouldn't leave if it wasn't urgent. There's a homicide scene I need to check out. I don't know if I told you before, but I spend most of my time at the precinct as a ballistics analyst."

Her fingers moved over the buttons on her sweater, closing the gaping fabric. She nodded quickly and he half wondered if she was more relieved than disappointed since things had escalated fast tonight.

"You're going to a murder scene. Now?" She rubbed her hands along her arms and he suspected his job creeped her out.

To his way of thinking there were two kinds of women—cop groupies and the ones who freaked out over the job. There were few and far between who could actually handle the way of life. Why did it bother him that she couldn't be one of the few? Hell, he hardly knew the woman beyond a few conversations.

And a peel-the-paint-off-the-walls kiss.

"There's ballistics evidence lodged in brick. The lead detective was hoping I could oversee the extraction to minimize any damage." The news would be in the papers by morning so he wasn't giving away state secrets.

"So the victim was shot." Her eyes flitted over to her newly replaced living room window and Warren realized why the murder scene visit had her spooked.

Guilt pinched him for wishing she was the kind of woman who wouldn't freak out over his work. Of course she would be uneasy when she'd had a bullet through her window. No doubt his life had hardened him to normal fears.

"This sounds like something more personal than what happened here. The victim was a porn star who met his end in a nightclub."

Instead of easing her mind, his words made her spine straighten.

"A porn star?"

He didn't know why it mattered, then remembered her ex-husband was a producer who'd gotten his start in low budget film that gave a few porn stars a legitimate vehicle. Would Tabitha have come in contact with anyone in adult film?

It seemed worth spilling a little more detail to find out if Tabitha knew anything that could be useful to Donata's case.

"Yeah. John de Milo." Warren didn't admit that he knew who the guy was. Warren hadn't personally checked out much in the way of X-rated films, but the names of the industry's stars seemed to come up in men's magazines.

Besides, he'd been reading an unsolved case file on an adult "reality" filmmaker allegedly based in Manhattan and de Milo's name had been mentioned in the report as an easygoing guy with wide-ranging industry connections.

"John?"

Her familiarity of the dead guy's given name disconcerted him.

"You know him?" He needed to leave, to get down to the crime scene. But this could be important to the investigation.

And it was damn well important to him.

"Yes. We moved in the same circles at different points in our careers. He always wanted to be a legitimate actor so we ended up at some of the same casting calls back when I was going that route." She stood, her long skirt sweeping around her legs with the sudden movement. "And I saw him just a few days ago on the set of a late-night, soft-core movie in the preproduction stages."

She bent to scratch Buster's head, waking the dog from a snooze. Immediately alert, the animal lifted himself to a sitting position, his tail swishing back and forth across the hardwood floor.

"What were you doing there? This was a film he was making?" He didn't know if he asked as a cop or as the man who'd just kissed her and wanted more.

Maybe a little of both.

"I assumed John was on site for the same reason I was.

To scope out the body double work. Then again, he might have just been friends with one of the actors. He was there with about ten other people, making a lot of noise while the production crew was framing the shots."

Warren didn't know what blew his mind more. That she knew a porn star or that she'd been considering taking soft-core work herself.

"You do work like this…often?" He wasn't about to make judgments. He'd grown up in a house full of people who'd made some seriously messed-up choices, so he wasn't the kind of guy to cast stones.

But he was curious.

"Never. I was called to the set under false pretenses because my contact sheet makes it very clear that I don't do that kind of work. Someone's idea of a joke maybe, but I was very uncomfortable. I wouldn't have stayed at all except that I didn't want to offend the director, who shoots a lot of high-paying commercial work."

That made more sense with what he knew about Tabitha. He remembered the way she'd clutched her robe around her neck when he'd arrived on her shoot earlier. She was obviously confident about her body and took pride in her work, but there was a sweetness about her he couldn't reconcile with openly sexual films. He didn't know where things were headed between them, but he was surprised to realize he wanted to know a hell of a lot more about her.

"We need to talk." Standing, he stalked across her small living room floor to stand eye-to-eye with her. "You want to keep Buster for me while I run downtown and I'll come by for him later?"

"That would be nice." She smiled and her eyes lit from within. If he stood there much longer, he'd catch fire, too.

And just like that, he wanted her all over again.

"Keep the dog. I'll be back in an hour. Two at the most." He couldn't keep his hands off her, his fingers grazing her hips with a possessiveness no man should feel toward a woman he'd only just met. But that kiss had him revved and ready for so much more.

He kissed her hard, savoring the taste of her until he had to tear himself away.

Her hair clung to his shoulder as he pulled back and he remembered he had taken it down while they'd been making out earlier. The mass of unruly red waves tumbled around her shoulders, taking her from delicately pretty to outrageously sexy.

"Okay." She nodded, smiled.

He kissed her again and forced himself to walk out. He hadn't been this gone on a woman since he'd been hell-bent determined to convince Melinda Cartwright to marry him. A colossal mistake despite his success in that particular quest.

The memory told him to proceed with caution, reminding him it probably wasn't wise of him to go back to Tabitha's place in the middle of the night. Especially now that she knew a murder victim.

As a good cop, he should question her further about that and maintain a certain professional distance. When the gunshot at her apartment looked like a stray bullet in a drive-by or the by-product of some street-related crime, Warren had figured there would be no ethical conflict about seeing her on a personal level.

John de Milo's murder might make that more complicated. But unwise or not, Warren was already counting the ways he could undress Tabitha Everhart.

SEX WITH WARREN.

Should she plead temporary insanity and renege on the whole deal?

Tabitha quit pacing her living room to weigh the thought. A good thing since all her nervous ambling was making Buster agitated. She'd taken him out for a walk an hour ago, but the dog was still as restless as her in Warren's absence. But maybe she could relax now that she'd come up with a way to back out of her bargain with Warren when he returned.

She could certainly prove the insanity defense. All she had to do was produce a few tabloid clippings from the year of her divorce and Warren would understand that she was unstable when it came to men. All the papers said so. Her jealous rages were legendary. No matter that there was only one public spat between her and Manny. Manny had a publicist, while she did not, so his spin on things got printed. No man in his right man would want to tangle with a woman like the press had made her out to be.

She could send the most intriguing man she'd ever met on his way without even having to bare a fraction of her real self. How neat and convenient for her.

Except that—in reality—she didn't want to send

Warren anywhere. Was it so wrong to hook up with a man for dessert only? Other women did it. She just had a hard time picturing how she could manage it since she'd never approached men or sex that way before. Sex had never been her strong suit anyhow, with her tendency to hit her peak too soon. Or at least, it had disconcerted her early boyfriends and pissed off Manny.

That was her first fear. But even if she and Warren got around that without too much embarrassment or frustration, then she had another worry. What if she got attached to him in spite of her best intentions? She ran the risk of getting her heart pummeled in this relationship, that wasn't a relationship anyhow.

Sinking down into the kitchen chair on the side of the small table she'd deemed her office space, Tabitha hoped if she sat still for two straight minutes maybe the dog would, too. Opening up her e-mail folder, she scratched the dog's head and waited for her messages to load while she wondered if she'd ever be brave enough to get involved with a man again.

Of course she would. Just not now, when her divorce was barely a year old. She hadn't simply weathered your average marital split. Hers had been a media explosion complete with passion, jealousy and betrayal. Was it any surprise she felt unsure of herself?

Her next relationship had to add up on paper and not just in her dreamy head. Manny had swept her off her feet with roses and dinners out, his extravagant lifestyle feeding her every stupid Cinderella fantasy. And surprise, surprise, she woke up three years down the road to discover his rampant adultery that no amount of marriage counseling could fix.

She'd breathed a huge sigh of relief when her doctor assured her she hadn't picked up any diseases from his infidelities. No way would she tread down the hasty fairy-tale path again with Warren just because he possessed enough sexual chemistry to turn her into a grinning idiot. On the other hand, she couldn't turn celibate just because she'd had a bad experience. Maybe as long as she stuck to the "no relationship" dictate she'd be okay.

Eyes scanning the short list of new messages that had landed in her inbox, Tabitha hoped to see good news from her agent and found only a handful of casting calls for the next day. No callbacks.

How would she pay this month's rent with no new jobs? She knew she could get enough temp jobs if push came to shove, but her pride resisted that avenue with all her education. She'd attended NYU's film school. She had classmates in Hollywood and working on Broadway. How could she suck so badly that she couldn't secure anything but body double work and the occasional foot modeling job? Thank God for her straight toes or she'd never pay the bills.

A mental black cloud threatened overhead but she refused to get sucked in. Her dream of directing had gotten offtrack during her marriage, but with persistence, the film industry would let her back in. Hanging around the scenes as a body double helped keep her ear to the ground until she pulled together the resources she needed to get back to her first professional love.

Working behind the camera.

Turning her attention to the rest of her e-mail, Tabitha clicked open a note from an unfamiliar address with the words *first take* in the screen name.

The note was short—just a couple of lines.

What's it like being in that apartment all alone without your new boyfriend to keep you safe?
Yours, Red.

She stopped breathing for one suspended moment. Told herself the note was some stupid new verbiage thrown on a million spam letters in the fashion of "why haven't you called me?" or a dozen other lines companies tossed into their subject headers these days to attract attention. The timing of this particular note just happened to coincide with her life.

Don't panic.

Tabitha checked the time the e-mail was sent, hoping it came over yesterday and she'd only just read it now. But the time said 9:20 p.m. Just fifteen minutes ago.

Who the hell was Red? She'd never met anyone that went by that name in her life.

She grabbed her cell phone off the kitchen counter while she clicked on the properties key for *first take*. No clues there. Just a run-of-the-mill private Hotmail account. No corporate name. Could *first take* refer to someone in the film industry?

Don't panic. Don't panic.

Buster barked, sensing her panic despite her best efforts. Thank God he was here.

Turning on her phone, she called a cab to meet her downstairs and then dialed Warren's precinct number, which he'd given her the night before. She didn't know if she'd be able to reach him in the field, but she'd far rather be with him at someone else's murder scene than stick around here alone and worry that she'd be next.

5

WHEN ONE OF THE PATROL COPS told Warren he had a visitor, Tabitha was the last person he expected to see on the other side of the crime scene tape. For a second, he wondered if he'd conjured her through sheer want since he'd been thinking about her twice as much as his job while he worked at the homicide site in Lower Manhattan.

But she didn't look quite like he'd left her at her apartment—with flushed cheeks and a sexy smile—as he led her toward the dance floor outside the tape. Tabitha followed him across the cavernous club, away from the backroom where John de Milo had been killed. She must have seen the address he'd written down when he took Donata's call. Her eyes were wide and frightened, her skin two shades paler than the starched tablecloths in the club's VIP section. Buster stood guardian at her thigh, the dog no doubt a ticket to entrance past the cop on street level since Buster was a fixture around the ballistics office.

"What's the matter? Are you okay?" He knew she couldn't have seen the body since it had been transported out twenty minutes ago.

He would have left then, too, except that Donata had been filling him in on an unsolved case she'd been working that might relate to de Milo's death. Apparently she thought his murder was linked to a reality-porn ring she'd started bringing down a few weeks ago. She'd arrested several of the promoters and the guys who'd been planting webcams in private homes for bedroom footage, but she hadn't nabbed the larger distributor of the films, someone rumored to have big industry contacts.

"Someone's watching my apartment." Tabitha pulled a crumpled piece of paper out of her coat pocket and handed it to him.

Donata, the lead investigator at the scene, came over from the VIP room and introduced herself to Tabitha while Warren unfolded the paper. The other cops on site were either in the backroom collecting evidence or questioning people who worked in the building, but Donata apparently wanted to check out Warren's visitor.

"An e-mail?" He read the paper in silence. "Red?"

"I don't know anyone by that name and I got it after you left," Tabitha interjected before Donata could speak. "I thought maybe it was just some dopey piece of spam, but the time frame fits with when you left and I freaked." She held Buster right next to her legs, her grip on the leash tight and white-knuckled, but to the dog's credit, Buster looked as though he understood he needed to be there.

"If he was watching the apartment, he could have followed you here." Warren passed off the paper to Donata and jogged over to the window that overlooked the street. "You took a cab?"

"Yes. I know we figured the bullet through my window was just a drive-by thing, but after I got the note I started to worry—what if it wasn't?"

Warren wondered the same thing since trouble seemed to be gravitating toward her.

"We can trace the server to see where it originated from," Donata offered, her soft voice echoing slightly around the empty dance floor of the vacant club. "Chances are he sent it from a public place, but even that much information would let us know how close he was at the time he sent the note."

Warren had the sinking feeling Tabitha's ex could be involved in this somehow. But what kind of dumbass signed a threatening note "Red" when his last name was Redding? Warren hadn't asked her about that, but he would when they were alone—more tactfully, of course.

"I don't like this." Warren guessed Tabitha was mixed up in something she didn't know anything about.

Or worse, she was mixed up in something she hadn't been completely honest about.

"We can increase the drive-by patrols in your area and alert the beat cops," Donata reassured her, stepping into professional mode a hell of a lot easier than Warren was able to with his brain on overload.

Of course, Warren knew there was more to connect Tabitha to danger than she did.

"I think you'd better consider a temporary move out of your apartment." He left the window, not seeing anyone suspicious outside but knowing that in a city like this, it was easy to hide in plain sight.

Especially when you were ducking cops who didn't have the slightest idea who to look for in a city filled with eight million people.

"I can't afford any kind of move." Tabitha was already shaking her head while Donata talked overtop of her.

"Don't you think that's a little excessive? She could install an alarm. Buy a dead bolt."

He walked away from the window, his footsteps echoing on the polished wood floor as he realized his attachment to Tabitha might be coming through loud and clear. His involvement with her could damage the career he'd worked so hard for if he wasn't careful.

"No." He withdrew a small plastic bag from his right jacket pocket and held it out for Donata and Tabitha to see. "I found another .38 slug here tonight, the same as the one recovered from Tabitha's apartment. There's a small mark on the side that looks like both bullets might have come from the same firing chamber."

"You think de Milo's murderer is stalking Tabitha?" Donata put a finer point on it, obviously thinking through the case aloud.

She didn't seem to think about how that blunt statement might scare Tabitha, but Warren watched as Tabitha's eyes rolled back. He caught her as she fainted.

Buster barked. Donata ran for water. How in the hell had he ended up in the middle of Tabitha's nightmare? But as he held her in his arms, feeling lush curves even through the barrier of her long wool coat as he lowered them both to the floor, he couldn't find it in himself to be sorry.

Melinda hadn't needed him for anything. A fact she

made clear many times during their marriage and finally hammered home by her affair that was the breaking point for him. Warren's remaining family might need him, but they didn't know enough to realize it since they thrived on dysfunction. Hell, even the police force didn't need him as a detective lately. His skills in ballistics were too valuable in-house to put him in the field most days, so he sat under fluorescent lights, connecting the dots in other detectives' cases while they collected all the field time and the glory that went with it.

But he could help Tabitha if he didn't let Red get the jump on him again. This woman needed him and he didn't plan to shuffle her off to anyone else in the department so he could stare at ballistics evidence all day.

This one case—one woman—he planned to handle himself.

"Please say I didn't just faint." Tabitha's voice drifted up from his lap and he realized she'd come around. Her cheek rested on his thigh, a visual that suddenly hit home for him now that she was conscious. And holy hell, wasn't that a sight?

Donata's shoes tapped their way across the floor with the water, but Warren noticed she left it at a discreet distance on a nearby table before tapping her way into the backroom again.

"You didn't just faint. You were clearly having an episode of extreme sexual need for me and you just fell in my arms." He squeezed her for emphasis, or maybe just because he could. She felt damn good to him and he thought a little distraction would be a good thing.

"I've never fainted once in my entire life." She lifted herself up, her breast brushing his arm for one incredible moment before she stood. "But then again, no one ever suggested a murderer was stalking me before."

She gave him a weak smile.

"I don't know anything for certain." He swiped away the memories of their couch encounter with an effort because focusing on her safety was more important than indulging a need for her that grew more insistent by the hour. "I need to study the slugs in the lab and see what comes up. But it pays to be cautious now that you're receiving questionable e-mail and you already had a connection to de Milo."

"I just said I knew him. Not well. I mean, I wouldn't call it a connection, necessarily." Her forehead wrinkled in earnest hope.

As if his believing her would make the threat go away.

"You travel in similar circles. Your paths have crossed." He rose, ready to get her out of here. "Either way, the danger exists and you need to be careful. I don't think it's a coincidence that your watcher is signing things with a nickname that bares striking resemblance to your husband's last name. No one ever calls him Red?"

"No. And wouldn't that be sort of foolish if he wanted to remain anonymous?"

"Maybe he doesn't care if you know it's him."

"It's not." She shook her head, mouth pulled into a tight frown.

"Okay, how about we get out of here and talk about this someplace else?"

He patted his jacket pocket to make sure the bullet was still there. He'd drop it off with the crime scene unit on the way out.

"It's late. I have an early call tomorrow." She sipped from the paper cup of water while Warren steered her toward the exit.

He tossed the bullet to one of the lab guys and watched while he stowed the bag with the rest of the evidence.

"I can go with you back to your apartment and make sure it's safe so you can pick up some clothes or whatever else you need for a few days. Do you have a friend you can stay with?"

She buttoned her coat and waited until he'd said good-night to a few patrol cops before she answered. The wind whipped down the street in the tunnel effect created by New York's tall buildings. The scent of take-out pizza and a nearby alley full of garbage bins carried on the gusty March breeze.

"I lost all my so-called friends in the divorce. Not that I blame them. Manny Redding can do more for an aspiring actress's career than I could, especially once he threatened to blackball me in the politest possible terms."

Warren slowed his step as they approached the corner to hail a cab. Buster stuck close to Tabitha even though Warren held the leash.

"A hotel?" He didn't want to push his own agenda, so he figured he'd offer all the polite venues first.

"Actually, I'm wading through a couple of lean months lately. I managed the hotel last night, but more than that is going to keep me from paying my rent."

She was short of options while a stalker watched her from the shadows. A stalker and possible murderer, for all he knew. This was definitely a bad time to convince her to come home with him.

Logically, he knew he should keep his distance even if he didn't get assigned to her case. And damn it, she sure as hell had one now.

But what choice did he have?

"You can't stay at your place." He thought he'd hit home that point again.

"I bought a dead bolt." She reached out to call over a taxi even though they hadn't come close to finishing this discussion. "And maybe you could loan me Buster for a few days."

She couldn't be serious.

"I've got a better idea. How about I loan you Buster *and* me while you stay at my place until we sort it all out?"

He opened the cab door for her and the dog jumped in first.

"So I can stay with you?" Tabitha grinned.

Damn but he was wading in deep with this woman.

"It's the best idea I've got."

"Thank you. I thought you'd never ask."

MAYBE THAT WAS terribly tacky to take a man up on an offer for shelter without so much as a polite protest. But Tabitha had seen enough horror movies to know the dumb chick who insisted on sleeping alone while a killer was on the loose was always the first to get whacked.

And Tabitha might have been naive when she

married Manny, but she was definitely not a dumb chick. She'd far rather wade through the potential sexual obstacles to sleeping at Warren's place than wake up with a gun in her face at her own apartment.

An involuntary shiver shook her whole body.

They were quiet on the short ride to his apartment, a ride made longer only because Warren asked the cabbie to take a detour in case Tabitha's place was being watched. They'd taken another detour from her apartment to his, even though they lived close.

"This is it." Warren pointed out his building as the cab rolled to a stop.

A sign advertising Caribbean food hung over a restaurant awning on the bottom floor. The place spilled over with people and old blues music, while a small neon placard over the door read simply Della's. Above the restaurant loomed about ten floors of what looked to be residences. The place had an unassuming air with no oversize numbers announcing the address, but the corner lot had to make the location more expensive than many of the neighboring buildings.

"You like Caribbean food?" she asked as he helped her from the cab. The scents wafting out of the building made her mouth water even though they had to be done serving by now. Her watch said it was almost midnight.

"Too spicy. But Della's serves Southern food, too. The crab cakes are incredible." He took her bag from the trunk and paid the driver before steering her toward a side entrance. "I can have something sent up if you're hungry. I know the owner and he's always got leftovers."

"That's okay. I've got to be on set early tomorrow for some leg shots."

"Leg shots?" He held the door for her and called the elevator.

"Close-ups for a steamy shower scene, I think. I need to keep up my connections in the film world until people feel certain that hiring me won't bring down the wrath of Manny Redding. For now, it's a paycheck." She slid under his arm into the elevator cabin and tried not to think about how they'd agreed to pick up where they left off earlier tonight before they realized she might be in danger.

Would Warren still want to take her up on that offer?

Her heart pounded at the thought.

"So you hope to get back into film in spite of the trouble your ex has caused for you? I pulled a few of the newspaper pieces on you last night for research on the case and I couldn't help but notice some of the controversy around the divorce."

That topic effectively squashed the heat inside her.

"Manny will deny it forever, but he told everyone who would listen not to hire me because I was difficult to work with. It doesn't matter that it's not true, he just never wanted to see me succeed in this business for reasons I still don't fully understand."

"Some guys can't handle a woman's success. Was he a jealous guy? Possessive?"

The elevator car arrived on the eighth floor and slid open, saving her from having to make eye contact.

"Yes, on both counts. I was shocked to realize how little I knew him after we tied the knot. He made a lot of excuses for why I should go back to school or help him with his career instead of pursuing my own goals in film. For a while I thought he was just trying to keep me ignorant of his affairs that I was growing to suspect. But it seemed like a moot point after the divorce and he still wanted to keep me out of the business."

Actually, she recognized now that Manny had wanted to be petty after a divorce that hit him in the ego. But to admit that to Warren would only make her feel worse that she'd been too blind to see it.

At Warren's door he set down her bag to open the locks and let her inside. The apartment was big by her standards. Eighteen hundred square feet maybe, which was a lot for an older building that hadn't been designed by today's hunger for floor space.

A small foyer led into a dining area straight ahead, with tall archways on either side for a living room and an office. Dark wainscoting made her think of an old library, while the rich burgundy wallpaper above the wooden panels stretched toward the dining room and then gave way to lighter colors. A leather sofa in the living room was littered with a little popcorn, but other than that, nothing screamed "bachelor." The whole apartment was quietly elegant and comfortable at the same time.

"Wow. Nice place."

"Thanks. My ex took all the good furniture, but after I threw a New Year's party for some neighbors last year, a couple of guys who own an antique shop up the street saw the place and decided to make my apartment their sideline project."

"They've done a great job." She'd been against hiring decorators for the ice castle Manny had bought, longing to put her own stamp on her home. But maybe if she'd had Warren's guys on the project she wouldn't have ended up living in a shroud-covered museum.

"There's an extra room this way." He carried her bag down the hall past the dining room and opened a door to a small space with guest bed, a weight bench and a TV. "Unfortunately this isn't anything the antique guys got a hold of, so the decor is fairly lackluster."

"It's perfect." She dropped her purse down on the weight bench and speculated what Warren looked like during his bench presses. Bad, bad idea. She licked her lips and tried to staunch the flow of sexy mental pictures featuring Warren sweaty and half-naked. "So you have an ex, too?"

The topic was guaranteed to cool things off until she got a handle on his expectations for tonight. And her own. She still wanted him with an intensity that surprised her, but the reality of seeing Warren at a murder scene and thinking she might be in danger had spun her emotions around so thoroughly she didn't know what to think.

"I was married for three years. She never liked that I was a cop even when we were dating, but when she stopped making noises about it, I figured she'd accepted the idea." He dragged the weight bench into the corner to give her more room and then shed his jacket, leaving her staring at him in a white shirt and a blue tie he'd loosened around his neck.

"She wanted you to quit your job?" Tabitha watched as he took the barbell off the bench and placed it on the floor, his muscles stretching the white cotton sleeves of his shirt.

And damned if her want for him wasn't overriding the unhappy conversation.

"Apparently my mother gave Melinda the idea that she'd talk me into the family investment firm eventually and then Melinda could have the lifestyle she preferred. Why she believed my mother when I'd told Melinda I would never go into any business bearing my father's name is beyond me." He straightened, the diamond stud in his ear winking in the lamplight. "She left three years ago and she's been married to a violinist for two and a half. She travels a lot. She's happy."

She sounded awful as far as Tabitha was concerned, but having been married to someone fairly awful herself, she kept the opinion quiet. Still, her mind kept tracking back to the fact that his family's business was investing. His background sounded more sophisticated than hers and that made her wary. Manny's social expectations of her had been one of the earliest marital war zones. But even though Tabitha's mother worked as a stock analyst now, she'd spent most of Tabitha's childhood embroiled in a bitter custody battle that left her broke, then had attended college while working two jobs to support them. Tabitha admired her mother's tenacity and was happy that she'd achieved her dreams to make a very secure living, but Tabitha didn't know her mother well and she didn't share her mother's financial stability.

"It would be nice if people could be honest and up front about what they wanted when they got married."

"Nobody's ever honest and up front. We just have to do our best to attune our bullshit meters so we can see through the lies."

"That's a very cynical view." She didn't want to admit that on her darker days, she'd shared the opinion.

She didn't want to remain a pessimist forever. Just until she got over the way Manny had screwed her.

"Hey, I happen to know I'm a really good guy. But even I haven't been honest and up front with you." He took a step closer and her heart jumped in reply.

"You haven't?" Had he found evidence at the murder scene that she should know about?

"No. You might think I offered you a place to stay for strictly honorable reasons, but that would be dishonest of me."

She warmed at his words, even knowing he wouldn't act on them tonight if she didn't want him to. He didn't move any closer but she could feel the flames flicker between them.

"What other reasons were you hiding?" She swore she didn't move her body, but her every cell seemed to strain toward him.

He stepped closer, the way she'd wanted to.

"My other reasons all had to do with the kiss you gave me back at your place and the implication that we might be repeating it soon, remember?" He dipped his head to her face since he'd lowered his voice as he spoke.

He didn't touch her, but his bristly jaw loomed near

enough that she could have licked it. The musky scent of his soap tempted her, making her knees weak with the urge to wrap herself around him.

"I think we implied more than that." Her heartbeat pounded loud in her ears at the memory of his hard male body pressed up against her.

"Did we? By all means, tell me what you think we suggested since I wouldn't want to be the one to presume too much." He stroked a fingertip up the side of her neck and watched her as she shivered in response to the feathery caress.

"I think there was a sense that next time we touched, we probably wouldn't be able to stop at just kissing. We said something about skipping dinner and heading straight for dessert."

Her eyelids fell to half-mast as her insides smoldered and her juices flowed hot for him. She didn't know how she could be thinking about sex with more interest than she had in years, given her day from hell, but she wanted Warren badly.

"Ah, Tabitha, I'm so glad to hear you say that." He nipped her ear with his teeth, his breath warming her neck as a bolt of desire hit her right between the thighs. "Because it just so happens I've got one hell of a sweet tooth."

6

If there was an ethical problem with him sleeping with Tabitha, Warren wasn't going to think about it until tomorrow.

He realized he was still staring at her, his hand gripping her shoulder as he looked down into her green eyes. She was so damn hot.

"I'm not good at sex." She blurted words he never would have expected to hear, her work as a body double at odds with the claim.

Her body was so amazing she showed it off on film. Men must have been drooling over her since she was a teenager. How could she feel inadequate when it came to sex?

Warren blinked. Forced himself to slow down when he'd been ready to start peeling off her skirt.

"What do you mean? I think the chemistry we're feeling is assurance enough the sex is going to be incredible." He kept his hands on her, massaging her shoulders through her sweater. He didn't want to lose the ground he'd gained with her and he knew she'd been feeling the same heat as him a moment ago.

"But I don't—finish easily. Or—more to the point with us—not always at the right time. And I just want you to know that up front so you're not disappointed or you don't think it has anything to do with you." Her cheeks tinged with color.

It would have everything to do with him if he couldn't make that happen for her, but he didn't say it out loud since she'd tensed up at the conversation. Her comment about having a sensitive trigger took on new meaning now. She apparently thought there were better times than others to hit her high note in the course of a bedroom encounter. He assumed orgasms at any time were welcomed by women everywhere.

"First of all, I promise not to have any expectations for how this is going to happen, okay? There's no time-table for what will take place tonight as far as I'm concerned, and no right time to do anything. So you couldn't possibly disappoint me."

A faint smile curved her lips.

"And second, sex doesn't have to have an end result. It's not a competitive sport, right? Anything that happens tonight is a bonus and it should be fun."

He hoped he said the right things to put her at ease. And not just because he didn't want to miss out on a chance to be with her, he realized. He hated the idea that a woman who'd lost so many other things in her divorce would have also lost her sexual confidence.

"Fun?" She lifted a brow. "I wouldn't call the itchy, crawl-out-of-my-skin feeling that I'm having right now *fun.*"

All at once his altruistic notions for the night fled. Beneath his hands her shoulders rose and fell with her breath, her body vibrantly alive and—he now knew— as hungry for him as he was for her.

"But it will be," he whispered, very ready to deliver on his promises. "Just you wait and see."

He bent to kiss her, lips grazing her mouth as gently as he could manage considering how much he ached for her. Sure it had been a long time for him, but banishing Tabitha's worries ranked as way more important than indulging what he wanted right now.

He kissed her that way for a long time, getting a feel for what she liked, exploring every nuance of her mouth to learn what pleased her best. The room was dim and he found himself longing to see more of her, to see her better than the shadowed bedroom would allow. She might be a body double in her work world, but she was the undisputed star of this show and he wanted to enjoy every last inch of her.

She was hot and sweet at the same time, her kisses tentative at first and then more aggressive as he prolonged them. He relished the feel of her fingers flexing restlessly against his chest, nails gently scraping through the dark cynicism he showed the rest of the world to the man he was beneath.

"More," she whispered as she broke the kiss, her eyes glinting with a feverish light he could see even through the shadows. "I'm ready for more."

"You and me both." He growled the words more fiercely than he'd intended, but it wasn't easy to pace himself when it had been a hell of a long time since he'd been with a woman. He bent to kiss her neck in the hollow of her throat and felt her pulse race beneath his lips.

Her fingers walked up his chest to curve around his neck, her warm skin smooth and soft. The scent of her surrounded him, intensified by the heat in the room, the heat of them.

He could see the dark intent in her eyes, the need that had chased away her reservations. He couldn't wait to blast every last vestige of that hesitation from her mind until she unraveled for him completely.

"No, you don't understand." Tabitha stared into Warren's eyes and willed him to feel what she was feeling. Sometime during the kiss she'd started to tremble inside and her body felt so close to that magical precipice she was almost scared to reveal it for fear of ruining their night together.

But she was being honest with him, damn it. And herself. She owed it to them both.

At his blank look, she picked up his hand from where it rested on her shoulder and moved it to cover her breast. Oh, yes. That felt delicious and she wanted more of his hands on her. There was no way he could miss the response of her body and the man needed to understand she was ready to go.

For as long as she felt this connection between them, she wanted to run with it. Revel in it. Wring every sweet second she could out of the feeling.

"I'm so close and I just need a little—"

She didn't even get to finish her words.

Warren understood what she wanted, his hand vanishing from her breast to slip underneath her skirt and up her thigh. The bold possessiveness of his hands made her legs quiver as he gripped her bottom with one hand, pulling her closer.

Heat suffused her cheeks. Her chest. Her thighs. She was so close and the fact that Warren seemed to anticipate her climax nudged her still closer to that sexual high. His warm fingers skimmed her panties as he whispered low sweet words in her ear. Words of wanting. Words about how hot she looked.

And *oooh*. There she went.

Her knees went out from under her and she wouldn't have been able to stand if not for his strong arms holding her up. He massaged every last devastating spasm out of her, his fingers never even dipping below her undies. The man played her like an instrument, his deft touch finding exactly what she wanted before she could even form the desire for herself.

"My God, you're beautiful." He'd spoken softly in her ear for some minutes, but that was the first statement she understood clearly after the most intense moments of her orgasm subsided.

The words soothed her soul, assuring her he wasn't mad about her oddly timed climax. He spoke to her like a man who was seriously turned on by it.

"I promise I'm going to be that good to you in return." She began to work on his shirt buttons, savoring each small release of fabric as she worked her way down his chest, revealing more and more of his hard male strength.

"You don't need to promise me anything. That was the sexiest thing I've ever seen." He slipped his hand out from under her skirt to return to her sweater, picking up where he left off with seamless thoroughness as he went about undressing her.

She ran her palm up the middle of his chest as she took his shirt off, taking pleasure from the freedom of access her work had given her.

His low groan rolled right through her, strengthening her determination to simply enjoy this chemistry between them for as long as it lasted. His fingers worked magic on her buttons, far faster than she'd managed with his, and in no time, her sweater slid off her shoulders to the guest room floor in a heap of creamy cashmere.

For a long moment they stood there in a silent face-off, their ragged breaths the only sound besides the traffic on the street below. She didn't feel exposed. No, she felt empowered with Warren's hot gaze on her, undressing her with his eyes.

"What are you thinking?" She nudged one bra strap over her shoulder, eager to shed every last scrap of clothing for his benefit.

For hers.

"I think I can have you naked in two seconds. Maybe less." His eyes burned with an inner heat as he seemed to assess the logistics of her clothing.

It struck her as ironic that she'd been forcing herself into the body double work for months to get more comfortable with herself again and to prove that she was desirable on some level, yet Warren had accomplished that in days. Hours, even. His desire for her meant so much more than capturing a fickle camera's lens.

His hands were on her in no time, unhooking the clasp of her bra and lowering the zipper on her skirt until everything fell away but her panties and the high-heeled boots she'd worn to ward of New York's chill. The combination of silk thong at her hips and leather on her legs felt deliciously naughty as she stepped out of her skirt, following him across the room to the daybed strewn with extra blankets and pillows folded in a jumble of navy-and-white piles.

He spun her around so the fronts of her thighs leaned into the mattress and her back arched against his chest. Her new view was a painting of a farm house on a river in the mountains, a pretty piece of artwork that didn't compare to her former view of Warren.

Her rump settled into his groin, alerting her to how much he'd been holding back. The heft of his shaft was unmistakable as he lined up against her backside, the tip of him nudging the small of her back. She didn't have enough time to explore the sensation, however, because he swept her hair to one side to kiss the back of her neck.

His tongue traced the curve of her spine there, sending ripples of sensation down her whole body. His hands wound around her to cup her breasts and tease the taut nipples. She melted into his arms, leaning into him, her hips grinding with more urgency. The warmth between her legs made her panties damp with want and she reached behind her to find his belt buckle.

Hands fumbling, she wrestled with the clasp, her job

made all the more difficult when he released her breasts to cover her belly with one broad palm. The ache in her womb clenched hard in response and she had to let go of his fly long enough to lower the zipper inch by tantalizing inch.

The climax that had blindsided her only minutes ago didn't take half the edge off her hunger for him. She wriggled against him, savoring the feel of him between her legs and wanting more.

"I brought a condom," she blurted, needing to feel him deep inside her before pleasure seized her all over again. This time when she came, she wanted him to be buried between her thighs.

She'd dropped the condom in her purse when she packed up her apartment earlier in a fit of hopeful optimism. Now, she dug into the small bag on the bed and flipped the packet onto the covers like a gauntlet.

He wasted no time in retrieving it. His hand dipped below her waist, pausing at the line where her thong met her skin. Her hands fluttered restlessly around his, not sure how much control she could relinquish without freezing up. In her experience, sex could be a battleground and she didn't want that to happen with Warren when he made her feel so incredibly good.

But before she could worry that thought to pieces, Warren cupped her sex in one broad palm. Her knees sagged beneath her and she fell forward into the bed, her body steadied by his other hand. Thoughts fled from her brain, chased out by an overload of pure sensation. Warren's grip on her waist, his fingers plucking at her sex through her soaked panties, his thighs burning an imprint on the backs of her… Those sensory impressions were all her mind could absorb. All she wanted to absorb.

He spread her legs with his knees, opening her to him, exposing her completely. She felt the ridge of his cock against her cleft and her nether lips swelled. Their positions made it impossible for her to see him, but somehow that seemed to help her forget everything but the pleasure of the act. She closed her eyes now to savor the feel of him, tugging aside her panties, fingers sliding easily along her wetness to circle her clit.

She stilled at the sudden onslaught of heady response, the tightness inside her almost foreign after being absent for so long. She could feel herself on the verge of a release she hadn't experienced in a staggeringly long time. A twinge of guilt pricked her conscience that she could feel this way now, for a man she'd only just met, when she hadn't been able to find release with her ex. But that niggling thought couldn't begin to slow the rapid build of delicious anticipation.

"Do you like that, Tabitha?" He steadied her hips as he aligned himself to take her and she could only nod mutely in response.

No wonder she'd been hard to please in bed, she thought vaguely. She couldn't even vocalize her wants or say what pleased her. Yet Warren seemed to know despite her silence, his seduction of her senses was so complete she could swear he knew what was in her head better than she did.

She reached back to guide him inside her, wanting

to contribute something to their joining but not quite knowing how. He shuddered when her hand stroked him, giving her the courage to circle the base of him as he edged his way into her.

A low groan wrenched free from her throat as she expanded by slow degrees to accommodate the breadth of him. The muscles of his thighs flexed hard as he held himself in check and she savored the way her body responded. He was all solid planes and ridges to her soft curves and she seemed to flow around him as he entered her fully.

The impact of his possession struck her then as she arched back into him. She'd allowed this man—a stranger in so many ways—to take her home, to take *her* in the most elemental fashion, giving him facets of herself she'd never shown to anyone before. There had to be a reason she hadn't been able to give over control like this before, but she didn't know what it was or why. She only knew she loved giving this sexy, powerful cop control tonight and her body responded to his dominance with undeniable pleasure.

His body curved around hers now, claiming her breasts with strong, kneading hands as he caressed and tweaked her aching nipples. The scent of him, of them, of sex, surrounded her, and she opened her eyes long enough to see the stark contrast of his hands, tanned even in the winter, against the pale skin of her belly before dipping into the trimmed thatch of red curls between her thighs. The scrap of lace that was her thong remained obediently to one side of her mound as he claimed her with each thrust.

Heart skipping sporadic beats in a race to send blood to all the highly sensitized regions of her body, Tabitha couldn't catch her breath as she watched him expose her clit to his questing fingers.

"Please," she murmured half to herself and half to him, not wanting the exquisite build to end. "Please, please, please."

"You please me, too, baby. Too much." He withdrew from her longer this time, drawing out the moment as he circled the tight nub where all her pleasure centered.

She fell forward into the pillows, unable to touch him or watch him or do anything else but feel what he did to her. It was so good, so lush, so decadently wicked she wanted to scream. And when he thrust into her again, impossibly hard and thick and filling her to bursting, she did scream. Waves of liquid pleasure flowed over her in a sensual tide, dragging her deep into uncharted terrain where she couldn't remember her own name but she could cry out his.

Only his.

The force of her release staggered her, her fingers clutching the nearest pillow as sweet spasms shook her. Warren went with her a moment later, his body surging deeply into hers one last time before he found his finish, too.

She wanted to weep with relief that she wasn't frigid, that she could have hot, incredible sex and find pleasure in the act. Her ex had made her doubt herself on so many levels it was tremendously rewarding to be able to disprove this one that was probably at the heart of many others.

"Thank you." She hadn't meant to necessarily speak the words aloud, but once it was out there, she was glad she had.

She needed to open up more. To speak her mind after holding her thoughts in for so long.

"The pleasure was all mine, believe me." He withdrew from her but managed to keep touching her even while he shoved the extra blankets off the bed and pulled one up to cover them as they laid down together.

She rolled to face him, the lamp beside the bed still allowing her to see his face even though it was long past midnight. She'd be tired for her shoot in the morning, but she couldn't find it in her heart to care.

Right now, all she wanted to do was revel in this feeling of completeness before it wore away. And she knew it wouldn't last. As good as it had been between them, she knew she wasn't ready for anything more after the way her marriage had devastated her heart. Her soul.

For the time being, great sex was enough. In fact, it might be exactly what she needed to get through the night now that she had good reason to believe someone wanted her dead.

7

WARREN WASN'T SURPRISED to wake up alone.

The clock near the guest bed said it was 5:00 a.m., but he could hear Tabitha in the next room opening kitchen cabinets and he could smell the coffee she'd made. At least she hadn't fled the apartment. Just his bed.

He showered in record time, counting on morning-after etiquette to keep her in his place until he was dressed. Then again, maybe she wasn't as wigged out by their time together as he'd been. As he brushed his teeth and swiped the fog off the bathroom mirror, he admitted to himself that he'd been caught off guard by the sense of connection he'd felt to Tabitha last night when they'd agreed on strictly no-strings.

"Desserts only" suited him better than she could ever guess since he hadn't intended a dinner invitation to become some kind of deep relationship. He'd always figured his effed up childhood had left him without the emotional capacity to have a serious commitment and his marriage to Melinda had proven it in no uncertain terms.

Besides, he'd appointed himself Tabitha's protector until he could pinpoint the creep who was watching her and developing a relationship with someone he was supposed to guard was pushing the boundaries of his personal ethics.

That had to be what was bugging him, he reasoned as he buttoned his shirt and followed the scent of coffee into the kitchen. He figured he was keyed up anyway because it had been a while since he'd played an active role in the field and the job was churning up the same old crap from the past that he would never fully put behind him.

That was another reason Melinda had left. A reason he hadn't shared with Tabitha since it would mean sharing so much more. Damn.

He walked past Buster still snoozing on the floor, since he'd taken the dog out in the middle of the night before he'd fallen asleep next to Tabitha. The dog's eyes opened enough to recognize Warren before sliding closed again.

"Morning." He spotted Tabitha in front of a bookcase in the living room. She wore a long purple skirt and white man's dress shirt and was studying a photograph of Warren and his brother.

The sucker punches from the past just kept coming. And why the hell did he have photos out anyway? The damn guys with the antique store had talked him into giving them some old pictures for their "too fabulous for words" frames and he—being a sucker who never had company anyway—had done it to shut them up.

"Morning." She smiled as she resituated the silver frame back on the shelf, her long hair spilling forward as she leaned over. "Just checking out the family album. This guy *has* to be related to you, right?"

She probably thought she was doing him a favor by making small talk about family so they didn't have to delve into the murky waters of where they stood with one another now. She had no idea what treacherous terrain she waded into with one simple question.

"He's my older brother. Andy." He tried to smile and hoped she'd change the subject. He even turned on his heel to grab a cup of coffee.

"Did he go into the family business?" she called as he disappeared into the kitchen. "I remember you said something about investments last night."

He didn't normally have to field many questions about his private life since his history was well-known around the precinct. Warren had been introduced to the local detective squad by the arresting officer who brought him in after the elder Vitalis was shot and killed. Warren's career ambitions had changed forever that night, shifting from finance—his father's dictate—to ballistics, thanks to his wrongful arrest.

"Actually, my brother was on the outs with my abusive father long before our father was murdered. By Andy, actually. His prison term is up next month." That was the short version of the story. The one that kept most people from pursuing the matter any deeper.

Warren sipped his coffee and waited for her to make polite excuses on her way out. Instead she stood there for a long moment, as if frozen, making him regret that he couldn't seem to soft-soap his past in more easy-to-digest doses.

"Your father abused you?" she said finally, surprising him by keying in on that particular fact as she picked up her mug from the coffee table next to her.

"My father was a bastard for too many reasons to recount at this hour, but my brother never stuck around long enough to make that trek into social services that might have helped us out. Andy's method of taking care of the problem was…a hell of a lot more devastating."

There were shades of truth in that statement, but he couldn't pick through them now with her watching him.

It had taken Warren a long time to forgive his brother and understand what he did. Especially since Andy had remained silent while Warren got picked up for the crime he didn't commit. Warren had been dissociating himself from the memories of his six-month stint in a juvenile detention center for a long time, so he possessed a certain amount of skill at the dispassionate retelling. The hell of juvie had made his father's beatings seem like a walk in the park.

An experience he'd spare her.

"Your poor brother. Poor you." Tabitha clutched her mug with both hands and traced the handle with her finger. "I'm so sorry you had to go through that."

Her sympathy seemed genuine enough when plenty of people looked at him like a social deviant for having been brought up in that kind of environment. But then, Warren figured the pop-psychology culture had given the general American public enough knowledge to understand you didn't survive stuff like that without sacrificing some parts of yourself. The worst criminals often came out of abusive situations.

But Tabitha didn't look at him as if he was a serial killer in the making and that—damn, that was nice. If Melinda had ever—

But those were stupid thoughts. Useless thoughts. Melinda hadn't wanted to hear anything about his past.

"That's not how most people see it. There was a huge outcry when my brother got off with just a fifteen-year sentence." Legions of his father's wealthy friends had sympathized with a peer whose ungrateful kid had—in their minds—only wanted to come in to his inheritance early.

None of them seemed to consider the circumstances behind the incident or the years of abuse that made Andy crack. And, Jesus, Warren didn't want to think about this shit today.

"I think I remember reading about that case, actually," she admitted. "I was still in junior high but I remember it being a big deal. Your brother is some kind of genius, right?"

A blood-deep bond with his brother made him smile at that, the truth of Andy's IQ part of the reason he hadn't been able to handle his home life. The genius factor had been an angle played up in the papers.

"He's brilliant. He finished high school early and got accepted into the top colleges for physics."

How different their lives would have been if Andy had simply taken a scholarship and left town. But the road lined with what-ifs was endless and Warren figured the time to change the subject was long overdue. He couldn't afford for her to ask any more questions.

"Can I give you a ride to work?" He set down his mug and reached for his keys, not surprised to realize he'd started sweating since his shower. He mopped his forehead and knew he couldn't blame it on the weather in mid-March.

Hell. He was still a mess after all these years. The darkness of those memories snuck up on him at the stupidest times, and threatened to reduce him to the cry-ass teenager he'd been back then.

"That's okay. You didn't think we were followed last night, right?" She shivered and rubbed her hands over her arms.

Warren acknowledged that while this change of conversation might be good for him, it probably sucked for her to be reminded that someone wanted to see her hurt.

"No one followed us." He'd made sure of that. "But if someone's been watching you, there's a good chance that person could be waiting for you at your job site today. This is the same place I met you yesterday, right?"

"No. I'll be in midtown at the studio today, but I don't want to put you to any more trouble. I know I probably overreacted by showing up outside a crime scene last night."

Which reminded him he'd have to answer to his department chief about that. No way the news of his visitor at a murder scene would have been kept quiet around the precinct. He'd have to squash any mutterings of unprofessional behavior first thing today and then bury himself in work. In fact, he'd been toying with the idea of bringing her ex in for questioning. As a big-shot producer, Manny Redding knew de Milo, and Tabitha, too.

"You have every right to be spooked and you're smart to be careful." He jingled the keys in his palm, grounding himself in the here and now to ward off the mental demons that had been let out of their cages for a few minutes this morning. "I'll drop you off on my way into work and swing by the set after I analyze the bullet I found last night. That might help us figure out if it's safe to go back to your place."

Her curt nod wasn't exactly enthusiastic, but he couldn't blame her for having mixed feelings about hanging out with a guy whose brother had gone on trial for attempted murder, a guy who hadn't said one word to her about their night together.

Crap.

"Thank you," she told him simply, picking up the small bag she'd brought with her from her apartment the night before. "I appreciate it."

"We need to talk later anyway." He shrugged into his coat and held hers out for her while she slid an arm into each sleeve.

The familiarity of the act landed another blow to his gut, a reminder that he was getting too close too fast when he didn't know much of anything about Tabitha except that she might be headed for a big bout of more publicity if it turned out someone wanted to hurt her…or worse.

She was young and beautiful with a scandal in her past—precisely the kind of target pseudojournalists loved for selling papers. And Warren had somehow ended up sleeping with her despite an intense dislike for the New York media.

Turning her in his arms, he kissed her hard since he didn't know how much longer he had with her before the press got hold of a story brewing. She held back for a moment, her lips unyielding in taut surprise at the intimate invasion.

But then her fingers flexed against his neck, lightly scratching the base of his scalp in response. She softened, warmed, melted beneath his lips and Warren was tempted to forget the need to be cautious all over again.

Too bad his refusal to look a situation in the eye was directly responsible for his brother's rash action nearly two decades ago.

He wouldn't make the same mistake again.

"TABITHA, YOU'RE ON."

The stylist waved her on to the bathroom shower set shortly before noon after a delayed shooting schedule had put the day's production scenes behind.

She had to get back into directing. Tabitha peeled off her robe before setting foot in front of the camera and felt every eye on her in the drafty studio as she bared herself in the nude body stocking that covered only the essentials. What was she doing? Maybe it was spending the night with Warren, but for some reason today she didn't feel like sharing her body with the camera.

She'd taken the body double work after her marriage

broke up to pay the bills and to thumb her nose at her controlling husband, who wanted to keep her under lock and key.

It seemed like a good idea at the time since she'd felt defiant and needed to call the shots for herself again.

This isn't me.

Not until today had it occurred to her how reactive she was being. Warren had endured so much worse in life than she had and he'd used his past to do something noble. Something that made a difference. But Tabitha had allowed her emotions to dictate something that wasn't right for her. And somehow it took sleeping with Warren Vitalis to make her realize it.

Was that being reactive, too? What kind of weak-willed wuss was she that she made changes because of the men in her life?

Gyrating to the music piped into the studio, she did her best to perform the sexy shower dance the script called for in a low-budget movie. The camera focused on her hips, her thighs, her naked back and the curve of her rump, as a light mist coated her skin. But the lens never took in her face. Never the real her.

She did her job mindlessly because it required no thought. What the hell had she gone to film school for if she was going to let her ex run her out of the industry?

"Cut!" The director's shout jarred her, freeing her from her shower dance that would appear on television with another actress's character.

Bad enough Tabitha had been living life without taking credit for her own ideas and talents. For the past year she hadn't even been taking credit for her own body that she'd worked damn hard to make peace with.

Fired up and eager to talk to Warren about her discovery, Tabitha had to stop herself from racing through her after-work clean-up to meet him. He'd called earlier, putting off his lunch hour until she'd finished her scene so that he could pick her up and see her home. Above and beyond the call of duty, but he'd insisted, saying he would arrive within the next—she checked her watch—half hour.

Ready to leave the set of *Total Exposure,* Tabitha changed into her street clothes and cinched the waist of her favorite purple skirt. She wasn't ten steps off the soundstage when she spotted a familiar figure coming toward her.

Two familiar figures.

Manny Redding and the bimbo girlfriend who had played a starring role in the end of Tabitha's marriage.

With nowhere to hide in the corridor of the cable television studios, Tabitha bared her teeth in a half grimace, half smile, and decided to brazen it out.

"Look, Manny darling, there's your ex-wife, the struggling actress," Evelyn Benson called in a voice that was meant to be heard. The auburn-haired former Playmate wore her typical do-me attire—a backless dress with a plunging halter neck that exposed cleavage of unfathomable depths between her jiggle-free breasts. "Are you still having to sell your body to make ends meet darling?"

Manny said nothing as he stared at her like a man scrutinizing subjects in a lineup, analyzing what she'd changed about herself. What aspects of her he didn't like now that she didn't listen to his wardrobe advice for every casting call. His fish-mouth expression suggested he disapproved.

Thank God she was doing something right.

"Hello, Evelyn." Tabitha's smile-grimace widened. "So sorry to see they botched your boob job. Thank goodness the new set balances out your hips at least, even if they are a little lopsided." She attempted a pitying gaze and walked faster, wanting no part of a catfight, but unwilling to let the woman's remark pass unchallenged.

"Wait a minute, Ev."

Tabitha recognized Manny's director voice from his days behind the camera, but she kept on walking up the corridor away from them.

"Tabitha." He used the same voice on her and she could hear his footsteps close behind her.

Mostly she wanted to avoid him because he was her cheating ex and she hated him for trying to shut her out of the industry, but in this quiet back hall, deserted except for the three of them, Tabitha remembered that Manny had reported her gun stolen without telling her about it. Had the weapon really been lifted? Or had he wanted the police to think the gun was missing because he had other plans for it?

She turned, knowing Warren would arrive soon. Plus gophers and set assistants ran through these halls all day even if the corridor happened to be empty right now.

"I'm meeting someone." She paused to look at her

watch even though she knew the time. If there was any chance Manny hated her enough to fire a shot into her apartment, she wanted to make it clear that he might get caught if he tried anything now. "Besides that, I thought we agreed to communicate strictly through our lawyers?"

He smoothed his silver-colored tie with the practiced hand of a perpetually well-groomed man. At one time, she'd loved the way he always worked to make a favorable impression, a quality she'd wished for her disorganized self. Only later did she see the sharp suits and weekly haircuts as facets of a supremely self-absorbed man.

That's when the midnight Häagen-Dazs binges had started to seem like such a good idea.

"Actually, I had to fire Braeden so I'll be sending you the name of my new attorney soon." He had the audacity to put a hand on her back as he reached her and Tabitha thought she'd scream.

Stepping out of his reach, she guessed Manny had only initiated contact to make Evelyn jealous. He was, after all, a master manipulator.

"Braeden O'Leary is your best friend." What kind of shark attorney could Manny have gotten if he let go of the guy who'd made Tabitha's life hell? She figured Braeden must be made of pure ice if he could have continued working with Manny after Manny stole Braeden's girlfriend. Evelyn was nothing if not ambitious.

"No matter. He's gone. Renewing some old contacts in the film business after a long time away from production." He shook his head as if to ward her off an unpleasant subject. "I hear you had some trouble at that flea bag dive you call home these days."

Tabitha tensed, grateful that at that moment she heard a door open into the back hall. A set assistant who looked all of twelve ran out into corridor, phone in one hand and a clipboard in the other as she rattled off twenty menu items for a lunch order. The reminder that this was a public building helped Tabitha breathe a little easier as her ex waited for her response.

"How do you know what goes on in my life?" Chills chased each other down her spine to think Manny could have sent her that e-mail, fully aware of her every move.

"The cops coming to see me was my first clue. Thanks for tossing my name on to the list of suspects, Tabitha." Cold fury turned his eyes a darker shade of blue. "Bad enough stupid de Milo gets himself offed the week I slap him with a lawsuit. Now you want to make me out to be some kind of drive-by gangster?"

Warren talked to Manny? Her heart pounded while Evelyn shouted down the hall that she was going to be late for her appointment if Manny didn't hurry up.

"I can't help what the police do." Nor, it seemed, did she have any advance warning of moves they might take that could create turmoil in her life.

"Be careful where you start pointing fingers, Tabitha. I've let you keep your body double work because it amuses Evelyn to see you peddle your wares to pay the rent, but I guarantee I can make that vanish, too, if you want to start trouble for me."

"Is that a threat?" Tabitha took a pen and paper out

from her purse. "Care to repeat it for me so I can get it down verbatim? I'm keeping records for the cops."

Manny growled, perhaps as a warm-up to another threat, but the door opened on the other end of the hall this time and Warren walked into the building. Commanding and so incredibly sexy, Warren looked as though he meant business. If Tabitha hadn't known him so well, she would have been running for cover at the dark look in his eyes.

Instead, the rush of relief was so great her knees wobbled for a moment before she took a deep breath to steel herself. She didn't know what she expected in a showdown between the man representing her past and the one in her present, but she hadn't expected Warren to stand toe-to-toe with Manny and breathe fire through his nose.

But that was pretty much the way the confrontation looked from her point of view as Warren's big, muscular body eclipsed Manny's slighter form.

"If you can't keep away from Tabitha, there are ways to restrain you that don't involve an order from a judge." Warren kept his voice icy and his body positioned between her and Manny while she stepped out of the way. "If I see you anywhere near her again, I'm going to show you the way of pain. You got me?"

Tabitha didn't hear Manny's answer, but she suspected he'd agreed to Warren's terms. Manny was an adulterous creep, but he wasn't stupid.

The encounter gave her a moment's pleasure in the vicarious revenge department since she would have loved to have knocked her ex into next year on more than one occasion. But as grateful as she was to have Warren intervene for her, she knew she couldn't allow it to become a habit. She'd never make it in New York as a director if she couldn't deliver her own ass kickings when needed.

8

WARREN HADN'T EXPECTED Tabitha to be thrilled that her ex was on his list of suspects for harassing her, but he hadn't expected her to go stone-cold silent on the subject, either.

Tabitha had barely spoken two consecutive words since they'd left the studios in midtown and now, winding their way through lunch-hour traffic toward his apartment, he wasn't sure how to handle the obvious tension in the car.

Had the sight of his inner badass freaked her out? He'd toned it down for her sake since he would have been all too glad to test the strength of her scumbag ex's jaw. Bastard.

"You might not want to take work that puts you in close proximity to your ex until we can be sure he's not the guy who's shooting through your window." He'd meant to say something more reassuring, but it bugged him that she'd been talking to the guy this afternoon in a quiet corner of the building.

"I had no idea he'd be there today, but even if I had, I can't let him dictate where I go and what I do. I've spent too long trying to scavenge up some control over my life to let him scare me into hiding now." She blinked and seemed to finally pull herself out of her unseeing gaze out the passenger window. "Where are we?"

He parked the car and stared at her across the console. Surely the Statue of Liberty in the water had to give the answer away, a sight visible despite the low-lying fog on the water.

"I thought you might appreciate a change of scenery after the last couple of days. How does a walk around Battery Park sound?"

"Oh. Sure." She peered around the half-deserted parking lot and Warren acknowledged he needed to be all the more careful in protecting her. She'd been so wrapped up in her thoughts she hadn't even noticed they were nowhere near her place.

A few minutes later they were walking along the Hudson River esplanade lined with black wrought-iron railings and dotted with public binocular stations for sightseeing. Patches of ice lingered on the water though the day was warm for March in New York. A gray sky overhead blocked any view of the sun, the moody dull light a permanent condition the past few days.

She'd pulled her hair into a rubber band on the way over, the long red mass snaking haphazardly over one shoulder. If she wore makeup for her job this morning she'd since scrubbed it off, her skin clean and creamy. He remembered how the freckles on her cheeks tasted, a sudden intense memory from the night before.

A memory he couldn't very well act on now when she could be in more danger than she ever guessed.

"There's no good way to put this." He'd been wrestling with how to tell her about his latest findings, but now that she'd had time to decompress after the run-in with Manny he had to fill her in. "The bullet that went through your window three nights ago was definitely fired from the same weapon used to kill John de Milo. I was able to confirm it this morning."

She halted in the middle of the sidewalk as if her feet had frozen to the ground. As the color drained from her cheeks he wished he was better with words and could have broken the news a little more smoothly. He stopped beside her, letting a young woman pushing a stroller go past them.

"What the hell does that mean?" Her words came out in a high-pitched whisper, as if she couldn't get enough air in her lungs to fuel her normal voice. "I'm next?"

"No. I'll make damn certain of that." He didn't even want her to think that way. After all she'd lost in the divorce, he couldn't stand to think she'd lose her independence now.

Or her life.

"But after someone took a shot at me, you're saying the next day the same person committed a murder." Her eyes took on a wild glint.

"No." He took her arms and spoke slowly to ward off the panic. "There's no way to know the same person fired the gun on both nights. I'm just saying the weapon that fired the shots were the same."

An important distinction from a cop's point of view, but by the roll of Tabitha's eyes, Warren guessed she was less than impressed. He steered her over to the iron railing out of the way of pedestrian traffic.

"Great. So maybe one psychotic criminal shot a bullet through my window one night and then his friend—also a psychotic criminal—borrowed the gun and shot someone the next night? Somehow that doesn't do much to ease my mind."

Her breath came in faster gulps and he steered her over to a wooden bench to take a seat before she hyperventilated. He'd been through the same kind of emotional ordeal when he'd been arrested and Warren hadn't possessed the skills for dealing with it then, either. What could he possibly offer Tabitha besides a promise of protection?

God knew he didn't have the emotional resources for any more than that.

"I can keep you safe." He knew situations such as this were exactly the reason cops should never get involved with the people they protected. It shifted all the priorities slightly off-center, making the job tougher. "I just need you to consider taking a little time off so we can—"

"I can't do that." She gripped the bench arm and turned her gaze out to the river, where chunks of ice swirled in odd patterns near the esplanade and a few boats made their way into the harbor.

"It would ensure your safety." Translation—she damn well had to do it.

"But since it would compromise my sanity, the trade-off doesn't work for me." She tightened the belt on a long gray overcoat trimmed in gold braid and antique-looking buttons.

The action accented her slender waist even beneath the bulky coat and he sucked in a breath at the memory of her underneath him the night before. What kind of pervert must he be to think about taking her to bed again when her life could be in danger?

"So we'll figure out something else." He didn't know how since he couldn't miss that much work to keep tabs on her during her jobs, but failing wasn't an option.

"Do you really think Manny could be involved?" She turned toward him and the wind snapped a strand of red hair free from her rubber band to blow across her cheek.

The softness of the question—the vulnerability revealed—hit him square in the solar plexus, knocking him back to reassess what he was doing with this woman still dealing with so much crap from her past.

The moment crystallized for him one important fact. He didn't want to hurt her, too.

He took a deep breath and tried to explain.

"Two of the detectives working the de Milo case went over to talk to him this morning but they didn't learn much other than that your ex-husband is a neat freak with a home office so organized he was able to produce a copy of the police stolen weapon report from over a year ago in a matter of seconds."

He didn't suggest that could mean Manny had reason to believe the gun would come back to haunt him so he'd kept the paper handy to cover his story that the piece had been reported missing. And it didn't help that Manny had been planning on suing de Milo for some long-ago deal gone bad when they'd invested in a film that never got made. The police were looking carefully at the picture that was X-rated, but hadn't ever been cast.

"Did the police ask where he'd been those nights?"

A tour group of school children moved past them in a long chain of backpacks and noise.

"Apparently he was at home with his live-in girlfriend."

"How convenient for him that he moved her in the house we used to share." Tabitha stared down at the water and waited for the old hurts about Evelyn to dig at her. Half a minute must have passed before she realized they didn't. She might not have forgiven Manny and Evelyn, but she'd done a good job forgetting about them.

Besides, she had bigger worries to contend with. Such as how was she going to stay alive with a killer possibly stalking her and how would she handle the sizzle factor between her and Warren Vitalis when her life was in shambles?

"Are you okay, Tabitha?" His hand curled around her shoulder and she wanted to sink into the strength of his arm.

But they weren't getting emotionally involved, damn it. And this was putting him in an unfair position since his role as a cop forced him to share news with her that would wrench anyone's insides out.

"Fine." She stepped out of his hold while she still had the strength to do so. "If anything, him having a live-in girlfriend makes him less likely to want to come after me, right? He's got the house, the money, the cars and a different woman to play his possessive games with, so I would think I'd be sort of a nonfactor in his world at this point."

How strange that it pleased her to be so unimportant.

"What about the girlfriend? Do you think she resents that it took her so long to take your place? Does she have any reason to hate you?"

Tabitha leaned back with her arms extended and then pulled herself straight again, hands gripping the rail while she considered the question. A ferry pulled out of dock and she thought about how many times she wished she could float away like that, leaving reality far behind.

"It's a well-known fact she and I mixed it up the night I found her playing tongue hockey with my husband when he was supposed to be refilling my champagne glass." A smile surprised her since it wasn't normally a fun topic for remembering. "Thank goodness I found out though. Even with being black-balled, it was totally worth it to pour Evelyn's appletini down the front of her dress."

"So you left Manny then. But it sounded to me like she's only been living in the house for a few weeks. Do you think she could resent that it's taken so long to move her in? Or that Manny hasn't married her? I hear she hadn't made a successful leap to the production side of the business after years as an actress."

He leaned on the iron rail and stared off into the distance at the Statue of Liberty barely visible through the cold haze over the water.

"None of that's my fault."

"I realize that. But she is a redhead. She could be the

'Red' of the note you received last night. People aren't always rational when it comes to affairs of the heart."

"You're telling me? I'm sleeping with a man I only just met and following my instincts for the first time in my whole life when I have no real reason to trust they'll serve me any better than logic and reason. Oh, did I mention I thought it would be a good idea to take up a new relationship while a psycho is stalking me?" She didn't want to consider that this might hurt his career. She'd gotten a strange vibe from his colleagues at the murder scene last night. But then, damn it, she'd known going there would be risky. "Trust me, I fully appreciate all the ways people lose their minds when they're under the influence of pheromones."

She needed to get out of here, to give herself a little breathing room, but she was at his mercy for a ride. For protection. Hell, she couldn't even go back to her apartment now that some lunatic was watching her.

"You regret getting close to me?"

"No." She paused. "I don't know. Maybe a little. This might sound crazy, but it makes it hard for me not to have anywhere to retreat since I'm staying with you. I'd really like to have my apartment back."

How could she respect the boundaries in a no-strings relationship when they were together all the time?

"What if we stop by your place and pick up a few more things now that we know you'll be out for longer than we planned?"

She should just say yes. He'd offered a smart, rational plan.

"I don't want to make you late for work."

He'd been so accommodating, giving up his lunch hour to pick her up at work and letting her spend the night at his place. But if she wasn't careful, she'd find herself caring about him.

"I think a trip over there is justified since I would have needed to follow up on the gunshot through your window anyhow. Come on."

What was there about a tall man with a commanding presence holding out his hand to her that ensured a shiver down her spine? His breath formed a white cloud in the cool, hazy air and she realized the thin fog had closed them in a private world even in a busy public domain.

She took his hand, expecting to follow him toward the car, but he pulled her into him, against him. His long, lean limbs and rock-hard…abs penetrated her consciousness as she stood very still, not wanting to break whatever spell had brought his body in close contact to hers again. She hadn't had enough time to revel in remembering their night together since she had to be on the set early today to put her body on display. She couldn't exactly hide her enthusiastic reaction to Warren.

"Don't regret this." He held her gaze for long seconds, his blue eyes hypnotizing her. "I've been living on autopilot for so long I forgot what it was like to be this attracted to someone. I don't want to lose that when I just found it."

The warmth of his body was giving her some serious impulses. Her heart thudded long and hard against her ribs.

"I'm definitely attracted to you, too, but you have to admit my life is a mess. I can't go home. I want to quit my job. I'm salivating over the cop who may or may not still think I have a murder weapon in my possession." Her whole world felt out of control. "I'm a mess."

She would have stepped away from him but the warmth of the day hovering above the cold river and melting snow made the haze around them the perfect camouflage to hide them from any unseen eyes.

"I don't think you have the .38 anymore. And for your information, a little disarray is sexy." He lifted a strand of hair off her nose to expose her face. "Besides, you're holding it all together pretty well considering the surprise of getting shot at, spied on and urged out of your home by the police. The week you've had would test anyone's mettle."

"I don't think I am holding it together, Warren, because in spite of the turmoil I still want to drag you back home and undress you. That doesn't sound like a smart, rational way to handle the situation. That sounds like an immature reaction for a woman with nympho tunnel vision."

She could tell she'd surprised him when he tipped his head back and laughed. Until that moment, she hadn't realized that she'd never heard the sound before.

"Trust me, we'll be discussing any and all possibilities of nymphomania in detail at my place over dessert." His gaze heated and melted her insides. "For now, we'd better clear a few more things out of your apartment before I have to go back to work. Fair enough?"

He slid an arm around her waist to steer her toward the parking area and Tabitha appreciated the change in direction of their conversation. The promise of another night with Warren chased away some of her cold fears and filled her with sultry want. A psycho might be watching her, but she would still have Warren in her bed to indulge her every pent-up fantasy.

And she wasn't letting him out of it for a very long time.

RED WATCHED THE COUPLE dance around each other in the middle of Battery Park as if they were the only ones in the world. As if no one was watching them thanks to Detective Vitalis's enviable driving skills.

Little did the good detective know, his behind-the-wheel maneuvers were a waste of time thanks to the wonders of global positioning technology. Slipping a GPS device into Tabitha's handbag had been ridiculously easy at the studio earlier. As long as she didn't switch purses or discover the innocuous-looking device, keeping tabs on her would take as much energy as flipping on the computer and checking the link.

A good thing since Red needed to know where Tabitha was staying in order to be a continued presence in her life. She must not have realized what information she possessed if the police hadn't made any arrests yet. But the possibility loomed.

She'd disappointed Red by sleeping with the detective so soon after they'd met. She'd made such a public drama out of the adultery in her marriage, yet she took up with a man she just met almost as soon as she laid eyes on the guy. That seemed hypocritical.

Possibly a little sleazy.

Maybe that's why Red felt compelled to kick things up a notch in this cat-and-mouse game today.

Walking slowly to the public transportation system while Tabitha and her friend reached their car, Red wondered if Tabitha had any idea how many more pieces her life could fragment into before all was said and done.

She looked happy for a moment, even if her eyes did glance side to side as she waited for the detective to open the car door. The anxious gesture was telling. And— truth be told—sort of satisfying after all the work Red had gone to lately to make Tabitha aware that she needed to be more careful.

But her idea of caution was to simply sleep with a cop. Clearly, the bombshell body double had no idea how much worse things were about to get.

9

FROM WHAT WARREN KNEW about stalker mentality, he didn't think the person following Tabitha would try anything while Warren was around. At least not today.

He checked the alleyway near her door as they walked alongside her building to make sure she'd be safe. If someone watched the building today, Warren would lose the person on the way back to his place. But Warren took a sort of peace from the fact that the stalker had only made contact through e-mail. In most cases, perpetrators used an ascending scale of harassment with letters and e-mails leading to phone calls and then contact—and only occasionally, violent contact.

The hair on the back of his neck rose at the thought as he made Tabitha let him walk into the apartment first. He moved through the rooms one by one, turning on lights and checking out the closets, a quick job since there wasn't much space off the living room save a small kitchen, bathroom and, finally, her bedroom.

He saved the bedroom for last since it was the farthest from the front entrance. Her bed was draped in dark netting pinned to an Indian-looking silk canopy. Bright pillows in patchwork silk and satin covered the bed, a setting fit for a harem. Or one supersexy redhead.

He smiled to himself now that he was certain they were alone in the apartment. Heading for the door to shout the all clear, he noticed a collage on the wall by her mirror, a jumble of newspaper clippings. It wasn't good manners to read whatever she'd posted on her bedroom wall and he wouldn't have lingered except that in the middle of the collage, someone had written in stark black magic marker:

Why do you have to make a spectacle of yourself? Remember the old days when you were content to blend in with the scenery?

Shit.

The jumble of newspaper clippings weren't anything she'd posted. Someone had pinned up most of the same articles Warren had read for himself online. These were the most negative articles about her and her divorce. The stalker had broken into her home.

"Warren?" Tabitha's voice called to him from the living room.

"It's all clear," he called back, wishing he didn't have to share this latest bit of news. For a woman who felt as though her privacy had already been violated, discovering her watcher had been here would take a toll. "But someone's been in the apartment since you packed up last night."

Silence followed, but her quick, quiet footsteps

brought her to his side almost instantly. He really needed to take some precautions to protect any evidence the intruder might have left, but first she had to see the collage on the very slim chance she'd posted the articles herself or had let a friend post them as a joke.

Her scent floated under his nose and he regretted that they hadn't met under different circumstances when they might have been able to keep things more simple. More elemental.

"This wasn't here last night." Her words hitched on a small tremor. "I've never seen half of these articles since I tried to avoid this stuff."

"No wonder." The articles had been intrusive on her private life at best and downright cruel at worst. He'd seen most of them online when he'd done his homework after meeting her, but a couple of these were new to him, too.

"I want to get out of here." Tabitha's arms were wrapped around her body, her shoulders rocking back and forth in a rhythmic motion.

He felt like an ass for standing here reading tabloid smut.

"I'll need to call this in so we can see if there are prints. I'll have it all taken down, but we need the lab guys to do it so we don't compromise the scene." He pulled out his phone and dialed the numbers to move things along. "I can take you to my place as soon as we get some backup and I can fill the guys in on what we're looking for, okay?"

Nodding, her expression looked far away and distant, an expression Warren remembered from that magazine article of her in the white living room, an expression that meant she was disconnecting in a big way. He hated to think she would retreat from everything—even him—if they couldn't get a handle on who was following her and why.

Yet he could understand the need to distance herself. If he could haul ass out of their personal relationship now, he would do it in a minute for both their sakes. His professional reputation—hell, his whole career—was on the line along with his personal sense of commitment to the force. He hadn't been investigating a case when he'd first propositioned Tabitha. But it had quickly turned into an investigation he couldn't ignore. And aside from what anyone in the NYPD thought about his investigative techniques, he had his own reasons for wanting to see justice tied to every bullet that was fired under his nose.

But there was no going back now. Even if their relationship was turning far more intense than they ever planned, he couldn't let her out of sight until he caught her stalker.

HER WHOLE LIFE was on display.

Tabitha sidestepped a uniformed officer in her living room, doing her best to stay out of their way even though there were four cops besides Warren crawling all over her place to collect evidence. They'd searched the alleyway outside and peered inside her trash bin in case the intruder had tossed something away. They did some sort of shadow-rubbing test on her notepad in her bedroom and only discovered her shopping list from last week had been the last thing written on the sheet of paper above. Now everyone in the room knew she bought Weight Watchers by the truckload and needed to restock her tampons. Charming.

Somehow stripping away her privacy seemed far more invasive than stripping away her clothes on the set. She'd steeled herself to bare her body. But in the wake of her hellish year, she hadn't quite reached the mental fortitude to have all her layers of personal protection dispatched. Her life under a microscope. The questions about her past and her crappy marriage were the worst, however. Didn't they understand she didn't want to rehash it all? That they were exploring down the wrong avenue by looking at her ex?

Although, she had to admit, the latest note from her stalker seemed to draw a connection to her past. A connection she didn't have the slightest idea how to understand.

Now she checked her phone messages with a cop standing over her, copying down a terse greeting from her mother and a request from Manny's attorney to meet with her.

Great.

What the hell did Braeden want with her now? The blood-sucking leech had already made sure Manny took everything in the divorce. She erased the messages with the cop's okay and then turned away from her machine.

Another detective headed her way and Tabitha froze, thinking maybe Warren wanted to double-team her on the questions. She remembered the woman—Detective Donata Casale—from the night she visited Warren outside the John de Milo murder scene.

"How are you holding up?" the lady cop asked, her petite stature and wild platinum blond curls debunking every stereotype Tabitha had about cops.

"I'm okay. Mystified, but okay." Tabitha tunneled her arms into the sleeves of a long sweater since her front door had been open ten different times in the past half hour.

"Meaning you don't have any guesses about who might have done this?" Detective Casale gestured toward the bedroom where other officers were brushing powders on the wall and examining the newspaper clippings.

"None."

"Even though—no offense—your ex seems to have it in for you?"

"None taken. And as much as I agree about my ex, this kind of thing isn't his style when he is skilled at exacting revenge in more socially acceptable forms, like slander in the papers and making sure all his colleagues know not to hire me."

A police radio squawked from another room at the same time someone's cell phone rang. Another officer passed through the hallway and out the front door. The noise and activity reminded her of the murder scene, creeping her out and making her all the more determined she wouldn't be next.

"But your stalker obviously doesn't like you being in the papers. Any secret admirers who might be upset with all that media attention?"

"Not that I know of. I haven't dated anyone since the divorce until—" Was it okay to mention her relationship with Warren? They hadn't really talked about that.

"Until Warren," Donata finished for her. She drew Tabitha over to the quietest corner of the living room. "He told me you're staying with him. And I think it's pissing off your stalker, who obviously knows your level of involvement since he e-mailed you about it last night."

Tabitha hadn't made that connection, but suddenly she felt more responsible for the whole mess.

"You think I should stop seeing Warren?"

"Hell, no." She flashed a humorless grin. "You couldn't have picked a better time to get involved with a detective, hon, because this guy sounds dangerous."

She nodded absently, hating the idea of hanging around Warren for such purely selfish reasons. But then again, she wouldn't admit to her growing affinity for the man who'd shown her so much pleasure and—if she was honest with herself—a hell of a lot more tenderness than she'd known in her life.

"Tabitha." Warren's voice called to her from the bedroom. "Can you take a look at this photo?"

She and Donata both hurried into the bedroom where the articles were in the process of coming off the wall to be bagged as evidence. One of the tabloid articles contained a large picture that hadn't been visible before under the collage of other pieces.

"This guy turning his head." He pointed to a tall man at the back of a table during a dinner party.

She remembered the event, remembered the meal with excruciating clarity since she'd begun to suspect Manny's affair with Evelyn during those martini-filled hours that were part business and part schmooze. She did recall being propositioned for a skin flick during the meal, a career low point that helped her realize she needed to make better headway on her goal to be behind the camera.

"That's John de Milo." She remembered him cracking more obnoxious jokes with each new round. "He didn't really have any connection to the business we were discussing that night, but he came to the dinner with Manny's attorney."

Donata leaned closer to the photo and frowned as she pointed to the young woman on John's right.

"I recognize this girl as one of the underage chicks who sold private shows from her bedroom when we were investigating the webcam scam last month."

She turned to Tabitha. "We still haven't located the distributor who's taking illegal webcam movies and mass-marketing them. You think there's any chance your ex could have been involved with underage porn?"

Underage porn? As in girls, not women? Tabitha hoped she wouldn't throw up, her stomach rolling in response. She'd known her ex had made a few skin flicks in the early days, but as far as she knew, he'd only hired adult actresses.

"If he is, you would have heard about it long ago from me. It's one thing for him to make my life a living hell, but if he ever did anything to compromise a minor with my knowledge, I would have retaliated in the most painful ways imaginable."

Donata hid a smile while the uniformed officer nearby cleared his throat. Warren held her gaze. Calm. Reassuring.

"There are no concrete leads showing a connection, but since de Milo and your ex both have ties to the industry and the girl in this photo prostituted herself for the same kinds of private shows that are being mass-marketed, I think we'll want to take a close look at everyone in this picture."

Donata nodded. "Maybe it's no coincidence that our guy is growing active now in the wake of all the arrests I've made in the last couple of weeks on the underage porn case. If there's a connection between de Milo's death and Tabitha's stalker, I think we need to find out who would be threatened by the two of them and why. He might think we're coming close to an answer if he's being bold enough to keep resurfacing in such a short span of time."

"I'm taking Tabitha out of the city for a few days," Warren announced, his gaze back on the collage of newspaper clippings. His eyes never even cut over to hers for a cursory questioning glance.

"I can't leave." She'd said it half to herself, so it was no surprise that no one heard her since the detectives burst into conversation as they divvied up responsibilities in the casework, agreeing that Warren should make the most of the time with Tabitha to question her about Manny's business associates while Donata looked at de Milo's background until lab results came back on the material the stalker left in Tabitha's apartment.

"Look, I understand I can't stay here. But is it really necessary to leave the whole city?" Tabitha's raised voice finally slid into a conversational hole.

Two sets of eyes turned toward her before the uniformed officers busied themselves with their work and Donata excused herself to speak with the officer who'd been making notes on the answering machine messages.

Leaving her and Warren staring at one another in a silent showdown she hadn't meant to create.

"You need to put distance between you and this guy." Warren's voice was steady and even, not exactly raised, but not exactly warm and fuzzy, either.

Not that she needed warm and fuzzy, damn it.

"That's why I was staying at your place." She had no choice but to lower her own voice since she was pretty sure that wasn't standard police procedure and she didn't know how much Warren would want the fact advertised.

"But that's not safe enough anymore now that this guy is ratcheting up his presence—and his threat level. He's not just a stalker with the *potential* for violence. He's already proven deadly." Warren allowed the last word to linger.

"I understand that." Although she had to admit that hearing Warren say it made it all the scarier. She'd gotten used to thinking that as long as she was with him, she'd be safe. "But I don't know how to make it work since I won't have a place to live next month if I don't show up for my jobs."

She wished she wasn't in that kind of predicament, but there it was. Her mother had made it clear to her a long time ago that she wasn't a source for help. Having worked her tail off to support her daughter and finance her education, Mom strictly subscribed to the idea of fixing your own problems. Sadly, the fact that Tabitha might have a deadly lunatic on her trail didn't sound like the kind of thing that would sway her mother in the least.

"I'm sure your landlord would rather receive a late check than have his apartment be the site of another crime scene since that can make a piece of real estate look damn undesirable." He slid his hand under her arm and guided her around the stack of oversize books that served as her end table. "I was sure to mention that to him, in fact, when I questioned him about seeing anyone around the building in the last twenty-four hours."

"You already talked to my landlord?" She tried not to raise her voice, but the conservative apartment owner and his wife had expressed doubts about having Tabitha in the building in the aftermath of her divorce. An obstacle she'd overcome by practically begging for a shot at the apartment.

Had Warren inadvertently guaranteed her eviction? She didn't mean to sound like an ingrate, but life had taught her that she needed to fight her own battles and forge her own path or she'd lose sight of her goals. For that matter, she could lose sight of herself.

"I damn well did." He picked up the bag she'd packed while waiting for the police to arrive. "And you can tell me all about why that sucks while we're in the car on the way to the Catskills."

WARREN WAS JUST AS GLAD Tabitha didn't take him up on his offer to argue about their trip on the way up Interstate 87. He had enough reservations of his own about this plan, but he couldn't see any other way to ensure her safety. When he pulled over at a convenience store outside of Rye, New York, he picked up a few groceries and called into the precinct to make sure his department chief understood the need for his absence.

The call had been tense since the lines of professional duty had blurred into his personal life. No doubt he'd hear more about this down the road and the possibility of facing a professional review committee made him tense. He'd hoped to avoid ever having his integrity questioned again in this lifetime.

By the time they got to their exit in the mountains, he was ready to set aside those concerns, however, and focus strictly on the job. Tabitha's safety came before everything else.

He flipped off the ignition in his driveway, hardly taking note of the house he'd neglected for the past six months as he let Buster out to run around the yard. Time to draw enough boundaries to get them through this enforced time together.

"Look." He turned in his seat to face her even though she stared resolutely out the windshield. "You obvi-

ously have trouble with anyone trying to take charge—
I get that."

"I'm not angry with you," she assured him. "I'm just
reeling with how to deal with this. The danger. The lack
of privacy. The inability to work. Things are pretty
upside down right now."

Amen to that.

"You know I'm not just telling you to get out of town
for the hell of it, right? I'm trying to keep you alive."

"I know. And I'm grateful. I'm just sorry that things
have gotten so convoluted between us since I'm sure
you don't bring many stalking victims to your mountain
place for safekeeping, do you?"

She might not have been aiming to hit him where he
lived, but she did a damn good job of it anyhow.

"I don't work in the field too often, Tabitha. They
keep me locked up in ballistics most of the time."

"But seriously. Have you ever put yourself out on a
limb like this for someone you were protecting?" Tilting
her head sideways, she seemed to assess him. The pile
of hair pinned up with a silver stick toppled cockeyed.

"No." Time to bail out of this conversation. They had
bigger problems to deal with than his work world. "But
I'm not backing out on you now."

"It would have been fun if we could have made good
on the idea of 'desserts only.'" She cracked a smile then.
"I'm sorry I turned out to be so much more trouble than
you bargained for."

"Don't you dare be sorry." He couldn't stop himself
from reaching for her, tucking a knuckle against her cheek

to stroke the silky soft skin. "We couldn't have known things were going to get so out of hand after that first bullet."

Or so he kept telling himself. He hated the idea that whoever was on her tail had surprised him at every turn. And yet, the stalker hadn't touched Tabitha. That in itself was a victory.

When she didn't say anything, he felt compelled to lighten the mood before he scared her even more.

"Besides—" he leaned closer to breathe in her scent "—no one said we had to give up dessert."

She shifted in her seat and his pulse kick-started at the warmth in her eyes. But despite how much he wanted her, he knew they couldn't go back to a strictly physical relationship. There was far more at stake here.

And with no dead bodies to distract them or stalkers showing up on her doorstep there'd be nothing to distract them from the meaningful morning-after conversations she'd tried to have with him last time.

As long as he kept the talk focused on her, he'd be fine. Because no way in hell was he walking down his own memory lane again anytime soon.

10

If she hadn't been so intimidated by Warren's obvious wealth and the power he could exercise over her life for the next few days, Tabitha would have been bowled over by the property Warren called a cabin that—to her mind—was more like a mansion.

"How many rooms are there?" She peered around another of the seemingly endless nooks and corridors in the sprawling historic farmhouse that looked as if it had been added on to with every successive generation. Buster ran around the front yard below, his excitement to be in the country obvious.

Warren's demeanor was far more subdued, however, and Tabitha tried not to take it personally. He was worried about the stalker on her heels, right? She hoped that was the cause of the tension in the car ride on the way up here and not a new awkwardness between them since they were suddenly sharing a house in the middle of nowhere.

"Eight real bedrooms. There are a few extra rooms that were joined together here and there so that some of the bedrooms have sitting rooms." He cracked a few of the windows in an upstairs hallway even though he'd turned on the heat. "It's kind of a strange layout, but the real estate lady told me it had character."

He shrugged as if to suggest that was a matter of opinion.

"Then what made *you* want it?" Tabitha could think of a hundred reasons she'd love a house like this—if she didn't need to work in the city. There were too many rooms for just one person. Maybe Warren wanted to bring friends here one day. Or did he dream of a future with a family to fill this big old place?

The idea touched her. Made her curious to know more about this man who seemed to keep to himself.

"No bad memories associated with the Catskills."

The hurt he didn't reveal communicated itself to her in a gut-clenching moment of empathy. She reached out to touch him but he slipped away to flip on light switches as he walked through a long hallway, subtly putting his back to her. Clearly, he didn't want to expound on the bad memories. It had to be tough for him to share the house with her, let alone his private thoughts about the place.

Willing to let the matter pass for now since she didn't relish talking about her own history—something she knew she'd have to do eventually—Tabitha wondered how long they could keep things light when their relationship was rolling out of control. Forcing herself to simply put one foot in front of the other, she admired the white walls with white wainscoting brightened by each silver mini candelabra that he lit.

Everything was simple and clean, different from his richly colored city apartment that his neighbors had helped him with. And while his apartment was pretty, this appealed to her even more. Which was funny since she'd hated every inch of her very white house that she'd shared with Manny. But here, even though a white cotton curtain fluttered on the window at the end of the hall, the floors were rich dark hardwood covered in bright braid rugs.

She had the feeling she could be herself here, that she could make a mess and it would still be okay. Not that she would, of course. But it was nice to know she had the option and that she wouldn't be accused of committing some horrible crime if she spilled her wine.

"Do you come up here often?" She looked out the window at the end of the hall as he turned into another room.

She couldn't see far in the darkened yard below, but Warren had turned on enough outdoor lights to illuminate a hill tumbling down toward a rock wall at the end of the property. She couldn't see the Hudson River on the other side of that wall, but he'd pointed it out to her when they drove in.

"A month in the summer and most weekends. I like the air up here for sleeping."

She followed the sound of his voice into the last room on this wing and discovered he had put her overnight bag on a painted wooden rocker just inside the door. Creamy cabbage roses covered the blue walls in a paper pattern that looked as if it could have been from the thirties even though the finish seemed fresh and crisp. A stoneware pitcher sat atop a high bureau underneath a map of the mountain region.

"How can you stay in the city knowing you could be here?"

"Married to the job." He shrugged as he stepped around her toward the door. "You want this room? It seemed like the most chick-friendly."

So they weren't sharing a room even after they'd slept together before. Clearly he needed to put some distance between them even though he'd claimed to still want her. Maybe this closeness freaked him out more than he cared to admit.

"Chick-friendly?" She pretended that his close pass to her body hadn't just seriously revved her engines even as his need for space hurt.

This time with Warren was going to be complicated.

"Flowers on the wall. Big bathroom." He pointed to one of the doors off the bedroom where she spotted a claw foot tub. "I'll be right next door. The rooms aren't directly connected, but they share a sleep porch."

She followed his gesture to another door on the outside wall.

"Do you ever sleep out there?" She walked toward the door, curious about anything that involved Warren and a bed.

"Not in March, but all the time in the summer."

She could tell he followed her by the way his voice came closer. Something about being isolated with Warren in a bedroom with no one for miles around stirred deep longings.

When she paused at the door, he reached around her, his scent and his warmth wrapping around her. With her back to him, she closed her eyes for a moment, drinking in the feel of standing so near.

The door stuck and he pulled the glass knob harder. She stepped back as it swung open suddenly, forcing her back into Warren's chest. A pleasant accident.

Nerve endings tingled while he steadied her, but he simply righted her and then gestured her through the open door.

"Go on out. I'll show you what it's like."

She hoped that wasn't all he showed her.

Taking a step out onto the covered porch Tabitha squinted into the dark. The lights from streetlamps on either side of the driveway illuminated much of the lawn, but since the porch was on the side of the house, most of the area remained in shadow. Plank walls about waist high anchored screens to the ceiling. A few tree branches brushed up against the screens and she could imagine when the leaves were out it would be like sleeping inside a tree house. Two empty bed frames had been pushed to the middle of the room that had a painted wooden floor.

"Are you cold?" He moved around her—in a hurry to put space between them again—and opened another door along the back wall of the sleep porch. "My bedroom is over here if—"

He trailed off as he pushed open that door and Tabitha couldn't stifle the urge to fill in the blank.

"Just in case I need anything in the middle of the

night." She smiled at the thought of all the things she might want from this man while she lay in her bed. "I am awfully fond of a back rub when I can't sleep."

He stopped his forward momentum, as if he couldn't very well ignore her or the heat simmering between them any longer. *Good.* She didn't care to be ignored.

"As enticing as that sounds, it might have to wait since I need to secure the house, touch base with the local police to let them know your situation and then question you about everything you know regarding your ex-husband's business."

The magic of being isolated in a charming mountain retreat evaporated like a soap bubble on a hot summer day. The attraction she felt to the man in front of her remained, but the sense of daring that she might indulge it vanished into thin air.

"Of course." She hoped her voice didn't ring with the panic she felt at the idea of digging through her past. "Why don't I go brew some coffee and turn on the interrogation lights for you? I'll meet you in the kitchen after I've had a chance to change."

She closed the door to his room and retraced her steps through the sleep porch that seemed darkly ominous without him beside her. She'd just have to shut down her feelings tonight to get through this—something this last year on her own had taught her to do all too well.

"Can I get you anything else?"

Three hours later, Warren switched off the espresso maker Tabitha had found in his kitchen while he'd been checking all the doors and windows around the house. He'd be wide awake until 2:00 a.m. after the pure caffeine they'd consumed over a conversation about Manny's business world.

How would he ever fill the night hours when a gorgeous woman slept next door to him? A gorgeous woman who'd made it clear she wouldn't mind a repeat performance of the night before.

"Actually, no thank you." She sat sprawled in the banquette on the far end of the kitchen where they'd been talking.

All he'd managed to discover was that everyone in Manny's life had been on one side or the other of a camera, but most of the guy's friends were producers and directors. Warren had a list of eight people he'd check out first, starting with the guy's new live-in—Evelyn.

"You sure? I bought a dazzling array of Pop-Tarts." He'd stopped at the store on the way into town but she hadn't given him many clues on what she liked.

Which—now that he thought about it—was reflective of Tabitha in a lot of ways. She didn't give up much about herself and the conversation at his kitchen table had been halting to say the least.

"No thanks. I have to be careful with junk food—not that I don't love Pop-Tarts." She tipped her head back on the black leather seat cushion.

"Your job is rough like that, I'll bet." He cleaned out the coffee carafe and put their mugs in the dishwasher, feeling her eyes on him.

Sitting across the table from her for so long had been

both tantalizing and torturous since he didn't want to open an expectation of emotional closeness he couldn't handle. And he knew damn well Tabitha was the kind of woman who would expect some kind of stronger connection with sex. Hell, she deserved that much.

"It's not my job so much as me. I'm a recovering bulimic and food can wind up a substitute for a lot of things if I'm not happy."

Drying his hands on a towel, he studied her slender form and pinup curves, her creamy skin and healthy hair, unable to picture her as ever having an eating disorder.

"You're not unhappy now, are you?" As soon as he asked, he realized how inane it sounded. "Sorry. I suppose you would be sort of unhappy with a stalker on your case and a cop who wants to take you hostage to keep you safe."

He slid into the seat across from her again, the wrought-iron chandelier over their heads casting a dim glow over the thick wooden table where she played with a blue beaded bracelet she'd removed from her wrist.

"I'm not unhappy, actually. Scared? Yes. But I'm getting along pretty well with my demons for right now. No need to exercise compulsively or starve myself. Being with you sort of levels things out of me, if that makes sense. I like how being around you—being at this house—makes me feel relaxed. Not uptight." She paused in spinning the bracelet to worry each bead between her fingers.

"You talked to a doctor about this, right?" He didn't know much about it, but he knew those kinds of disorders could take a huge toll on physical health.

"Many times." She put down the bracelet again and sighed. "I was diagnosed as a teenager when I took to binge eating. When my mother saw me putting on weight, she couldn't race me to the doctor fast enough, but she wasn't too happy with the diagnosis, suggesting I might be trying to take control of some part of my life in an ultracontrolling household."

Warren whistled softly between his teeth.

"I can see where that might not go over well."

"I'm sure you can imagine it got worse after that. I was out of the house by the time I was seventeen and on my own for a few years before I met Manny. Food helped me deal with emotional situations."

"You met Manny in film school, right?"

"Yes. He seemed great at first. We shared a lot of interests in film. It wasn't until a few years later that I realized I'd married my mother. Whoops." She thunked the flat of her palm against her forehead. "Hell of a realization. And my first clue was that I started bingeing again. In a couple of months I was back on the merry-go-round of exercise and dieting. I hit a fast downward spiral because I felt like crap about myself."

"How does your work factor in? Does it make it tougher to eat well?" He remembered seeing some of the extravagant spreads the studios laid out for employees on location sets during his years as a beat cop and he knew they spared no expense.

"It's probably been good for me since the intense focus on the physical forces me to be kinder to myself. And it helps that I can put me first now instead of my ex-husband, who was a big personality and needed to be the center of everything. This year has been all about finding balance on a lot of levels."

He had to admire that about her. He'd never forgotten his six-month lockup that had put him in close contact with society's most severely unbalanced people. Tabitha had battled hard for the self-awareness that kept her strong.

She jammed her beads back on her hand while he shoved aside his notes. Any questions he had for her now were based in a more personal interest.

"So did you ever iron things out with your mom?" He reached over the table to take her hand in his, running his thumb along the smooth knuckles dotted with light freckles.

"Not really. We talk about once a month when we're on speaking terms, which hasn't been often since my divorce. She's a stock analyst with a very driven Type A personality. She never married my father since he wasn't in her career plans and he seemed just as glad to take the first boat back to Ireland after an extended trip to the States. He started writing me letters when I moved out of my mom's house but he's never expressed any great interest in meeting me." She shrugged as though her father's lazy-ass parenting hadn't hurt her one way or another.

Outside the wind kicked up, banging a loose shutter against the side of the house somewhere upstairs. He'd forgotten all the flaws of the house when he'd decided to bring her here, thinking only about the benefits of distance from the city.

"His loss." Warren couldn't imagine what kind of idiot would turn his back on his daughter, especially a woman like this one who'd fought so hard for the sense of self-worth everyone around her seemed determined to trash.

"That's what I like to think." She straightened in her seat, the leather cushion squeaking softly as she shifted. "But I should get some sleep or at least leave you in peace if we're finished with the questions about Manny."

Only then did Warren realize he still held her hand. Releasing her took an effort even though he knew it would be wisest to let her go.

"I'll walk you up." He stood, knowing it would present an even bigger challenge to leave her at her door tonight when every male impulse he possessed called out to him to show her exactly how incredible she was, even if her ex and her controlling mama were too stupid to see it.

"Do you think that's a good idea?" She raked a hand through her flame-red hair and unsettled the halfhearted knot she'd tied it in at the back of her head. "I mean, I'm not one bit tired after the espresso and I have to confess I'm more interested in jumping you than going to bed. I just thought it might make it easier to part company before we got too comfortable down here since my mind has already been wandering in the…ah…intimate direction."

Oh, hell.

The big country kitchen couldn't have seemed smaller in that moment, the small chandelier overhead casting a seductive glow over Tabitha's pale skin. The tailored white shirt she wore seemed anything but conservative since the last button was fastened a half inch above her cleavage and the space gapped enticingly over one creamy mound.

Besides, she wanted him.

"I don't know if walking you upstairs is a good idea or not since, frankly, I just forgot my own name." His mouth watered as his gaze slid to her soft lips and he remembered their taste with painful clarity.

"I'm pretty sure you're trying to stay away from me," she reminded him, her wide eyes revealing a vulnerability he hadn't meant to put there.

"Then it must be for your own good since I'm damn certain it's not what I want. I'm still game to keep things as easy as we can make them." He wondered if science had ever proven that the logic portion of the human brain ceased to function when exposed to high temperatures.

He figured his gray matter would provide the proof right this second.

"You don't think that keeping things simple is a losing cause?" She placed a hand on his chest and the gesture seemed to torch his insides.

The walls were closing in on him along with memories of how good they'd been together the night before.

"I never lose." His hands found their way to Tabitha's shoulders, where he imagined he might hold her off, but the feel of her had him massaging her through the cotton instead.

"Excellent. I've got the personal guarantee of a city

cop. New York's finest." She licked her lips with slow deliberation and he found his gaze fastened to her glistening mouth. "As long as you're game, I've got a few…oh, let's call them sensual wishes I've been hoping you'd take under consideration."

Indulge Tabitha's desires?

Yes. Right. Made total sense.

He'd figure out a way to keep things simple tomorrow. For right now, he planned to give this woman everything in the world she wanted. Everything she deserved, at least for a night.

"Okay, Tabitha." He worked the knot out of her hair and watched the mass of red waves spill over her shoulders. "Why don't you tell me your first wish?"

11

TABITHA STOOD utterly still in Warren's kitchen and savored the feel of dark desire wound up with a deep joy foreign to her until she'd met him. Looking at him pleased her. Fascinated her. His angular face lacked any kind of particular beauty and yet she found she couldn't look away.

She wanted him with a need that left her breathless, and yet the wanting was almost as delicious as knowing she'd have him. Soon. That state of delayed fulfillment stirred a hot tension inside her, a pleasurable ache tempered only by the knowledge that he might regret this tomorrow.

And even though she wanted to know why, to understand what held him back, she couldn't silence the selfish urge to accept what he could give her without questioning it any further.

"I wish you'd kiss me like you couldn't get enough of me," she confided finally, almost dizzy with the anticipation of this powerful, compelling man doing her bidding for the night.

A heady prospect.

"You're way too easy to please." His hands crept over her collarbone to slide under her shirt. "You know I would have undressed you with my teeth or licked whipped cream off your breasts or tied you to my bedposts if you asked me to, right?"

Her eyes flew open wide to see his face, to gauge if he was kidding.

He wasn't.

A mental picture ensued that was so vivid she didn't think she'd ever get it out of her head. What would it be like to be subject to Warren's every whim? What dark desires did this complicated man hide from her now that he might play out if she was bound to his bed? Shivers chased each other up her spine and back down again, lingering low on her hips to ignite an ache between her thighs.

"Oh." Her heart pounded a fervent answer to his suggestions and she wondered how many women he'd tied to his bed in the past. "I thought you were trying to… um…put some distance between us. You know, separate rooms and everything."

"I was trying not to make you feel like I was moving too fast. I wouldn't want to assume that—hell. I just didn't want to make assumptions."

She wasn't sure that he admitted the whole truth on that score. But maybe that was as much of the truth as he could handle right now with the way things had escalated between them. Besides, she refused to overthink this when he was finally getting close to her.

"Then I'll keep the whipped cream offer in mind.

Remember the kiss is only my *first* wish." She wanted him to keep that in mind.

Her mouth watered for him as she mentally undressed him. She wanted to trace every muscle in his powerful body, memorize the texture of his hot skin over solid muscle.

"Good." His thick fingers nudged one bra strap off her shoulder, the silky fabric teasing her skin and making her ultra-aware of that tiny patch of flesh he'd bared. "Then be thinking about your next wish while I grant this first one. And let me say that I'll consider the kiss a failure if it doesn't inspire something infinitely racier."

His eyes glittered blue and dangerous in the lamplight, as if daring her to dream up the best possible ways to put his rock-hard body to work.

She meant to nod. To say okay. To show her agreement somehow, but she seemed mesmerized by the chemistry firing between them as he leaned closer. Closer.

Covering her lips with his, he tasted her with the easy confidence of a man who knew his way around a kiss. She savored the way their mouths merged and melded, the heat intensifying with each stroke of his tongue as he teased his way inside. He tipped her head back to improve his angle, or perhaps just to exert more control over the kiss. She gladly allowed him to steer her whole body backward across the kitchen until she felt the refrigerator at her back. The soft thunk of her butt into the appliance was eased by the feel of Warren's body pressing into hers, his hips dominating hers as he kissed harder, deeper.

Her knees wobbled, leaving her with no choice but to wrap her arms around his neck and hold on tight. Somehow he'd unbuttoned her blouse to clear his path to her breasts and he fingered a taut nipple through the thin layer of silk and Lycra that made up her camisole bra.

Her fingers practically pawed at him as she explored the bristly hair at the base of his scalp. The thick cords of his neck hinted at a strength she wanted to experience firsthand tonight.

Her shirt slid halfway down her shoulders as he cupped a breast in his palm, lifting her out of the bra cup to gain full access. He tweaked the crest between his thumb and forefinger at the same time he nipped her lower lip between his teeth and she practically convulsed with the sharp contraction of her feminine muscles.

She arched one leg high alongside his, her knee parallel to his waist in a gesture that opened her to his erection straining the fabric of his trousers. The coarse wool tickled her through her panties but the hard strength of him underneath the material made the slight discomfort delightfully worthwhile.

He hauled up her skirt with one hand and tossed the extra fabric over his arm to keep it out of the way. A slight draft hit her bare legs, reminding her that she exposed everything to him and they hadn't even left the kitchen. The refrigerator hummed a gentle rhythm at her back, the rumble of the old appliance providing a small thrill.

And still his kiss went on. She clutched at his shirt, needing to feel more of him and not knowing how to ask. She'd have to break the kiss if she wanted to request any more wishes, and she couldn't begin to scavenge the kind of resources she'd need to end the best lip-lock of her life. She'd wanted to be kissed as though he couldn't get enough of her and oh, man, he was doing an amazing, toe-curling job with that.

Taking the matter of his clothes into her own hands, she pulled fabric and bunched material until she had his shirt mostly off and his zipper at half-mast. He stopped her then, pausing the kiss just long enough to tug his wallet from his pocket and hand it to her.

"Condom. Front and center."

It took her a moment to process the words while he bent to kiss his way down her neck and into the *V* of her cleavage. Her camisole acted like a push-up bra with her breasts spilling out over the top of it, putting the mounds within easy tasting distance. He circled one nipple with his tongue while she dug through the wallet and past his twenties to find a foil packet.

Jackpot.

The wallet fell to the floor along with a strip of foil she tore off in order to free the condom. Her heart hammered in her chest, but not from nervousness about whether she'd reach her orgasm at the right time. No, her erratic pulse was strictly the result of smoldering hunger for Warren and for all the things he could do to her.

He released her breast to look her in the eye for one blistering hot second, his gaze raking over her with an intensity that hadn't been there earlier. For a moment she saw his nobler impulses stripped and the emotion remaining was something frightening and thrilling at the same time.

Her hands shook as she unzipped his pants the rest of the way and freed him from the confines of his boxers. His cock was smooth and hot to the touch and she eased the condom over him with some difficulty since the head of him bobbed and strained closer to her thighs. When she had him fully sheathed he yanked her panties off her hips with the same ease she ripped price tags off new clothes. One tug and her panties were on the kitchen floor, baring her slick heat to his questing fingers.

He kissed her then, covering her lips with his the way she wanted him to cover the rest of her. She teased his outer thigh with a shift of her leg against his and he answered by lifting her leg higher, making her very aware of her vulnerability to him. He could have her any way he wanted to and the knowledge sent a fresh twinge between her legs.

She wanted him so badly she writhed against him, desperate for the feel of his cock against her swollen labia. He trapped her hands in his against the refrigerator, holding her perfectly still as he kissed her and only then did he allow the tip of him to brush her clit. That small contact incited a strangled cry in her throat, a mewling yelp that bore no resemblance to her speaking voice.

If her hands had been free she would have helped guide him inside her, but instead he kissed and teased her, tormenting them both with glancing touches that built anticipation to a perilous level. Tabitha's whole body trembled by now, her every breath and every shuddering sigh focused on the exquisite pleasure of almost-touches that never gave her the full measure of man she wanted.

The scent of skin and sex and espresso permeated the kitchen while the sounds of their breathing seemed magnified in the quiet house. She longed and wanted, hungered and cried out for him, until finally he released her hands to take hold of her legs. He fit them both around his waist, holding her up with his strength and the leverage of the fridge. Her widespread thighs splayed her sex to his erection for a pulse-pounding moment before he positioned himself to enter her. Uncaring of her position, she tilted her hips to receive him, trusting him to hang on to her even if she didn't make it easy.

And oh, baby, was her trust well-placed. Warren twisted and angled and bent his body around hers to fine-tune the thrust.

He cupped her butt cheeks in his hands, shifting his position while he held her steady. Her breasts flattened against his chest, her body curving and softening to accommodate his hard angles and masculine strength.

Tension built inside her, the slow windup to a climax still taking her by surprise even if he had delivered that same powerful jolt to her body the night before. How did Warren know her so much better than she knew herself? How could he have predicted what things would turn her on to that degree when she didn't have any idea she wanted to be taken hard and fast against a refrigerator?

Just the thought of what they were doing, of how wildly abandoned she must look right now, was enough to push her to the final level of sexual frenzy. She clawed at his shoulders, needing to anchor herself before the bottom fell out of her world. Finding some purchase in the ripple of muscle along his biceps, she held on to him while her back arched helplessly as the tide of sensations swept through her, pounding her body like the waves of an incoming tide.

Warren's body froze the next moment, a stony paralyzed second as he found his fulfillment. She didn't know how long the moment lasted for him, but her reward went on and on. She screamed so loud the dog barked at the door outside, but she couldn't even call a soothing cry to the poor animal since her release had robbed her of all ability to speak, think or move for the next two minutes. She only managed to breathe in and breathe out, the rhythmic motion eventually forcing her heart rate to slow.

When awareness returned she peeled herself off the refrigerator while Warren straightened his clothes and gently pulled her bra straps back into place on her shoulders. The tender gesture caught her by surprise coming from a man who didn't want any kind of deeper relationship. Was she being a wishful female to read into that gesture?

While she saw so much strength of character and flat-out honor in Warren, that didn't change the fact that he didn't want to wade into emotional terrain with her.

That meant she needed to stick to their original bargain. No strings. She'd walk away from their incredible encounter now if it killed her. She wouldn't let him think she was waiting for any heartfelt declarations or impassioned offer to spend the night in his bed.

"You sure know how to fulfill a woman's expectations." She hoped her smile came across as flirtatious. "That was one kiss I won't forget."

Smoothing her skirt, she stuffed her torn panties in her pocket and then buttoned two buttons on her blouse, just enough to make her feel a little less exposed. God knew the sex against the refrigerator was making her feel plenty vulnerable already.

"I meant to ask you what else you wanted—" he started, but she didn't think she could remain her cool distance if he went there so she spoke over top of him.

"I think you must have telepathically intuited my other wishes because you don't hear me wanting for anything more." Except maybe to be wrapped in his arms right now.

Had he been this closed-off with his wife? she wondered. Tabitha couldn't help a moment of empathy with the woman now that she'd seen how it felt to make love to him and still feel like she hardly knew him.

"Tabitha—" He hesitated, his gaze dark and troubled. But he must have changed his mind about whatever he would have said because he settled for sliding his arm around her instead. "Let me walk you upstairs."

She nodded tightly, afraid to say much or her wound-up emotions might spill out through her words. They walked up the stairs in silence, pausing only to let Buster inside for the night. Warren seemed to be heading for her room and a moment of panic seized her. Maybe Warren had a point about keeping separate rooms to give them a corner to retreat to at the end of the day, at least until they figured out where this relationship was headed.

By the time they reached her room, she took the coward's way out and, after kissing him on the cheek, sprinted through her door with a falsely cheery good night.

He was an ass.

Warren wiped his gritty eyes as he shifted his gaze from his laptop to the rising sun outside his bedroom window. He'd come to that same inescapable conclusion the night before when Tabitha had all but run screaming from him in a painfully obvious attempt to assure him she didn't need a lot of TLC with sex and that she could keep it light and casual between them. But he'd spent hours ignoring the conclusion since he didn't like the picture that painted of him or the position he'd put Tabitha in because he couldn't keep his hands to himself.

He never tired of watching the sunrise creep up over the Hudson, having removed the blinds in this room because he liked seeing each dawn firsthand, a perpetual reminder that no matter how crappy the day before had been, each day gave him a new shot at getting it right. He hated to think how many days of his life he'd spent pinning hopes on a stupid sunrise instead of taking steps to fix the biggest problem he faced most days.

Him.

He slapped his hand on the small writing desk, making his papers jump. Now wasn't a good time to get down on himself about his lack of relationship skills, since Tabitha was in danger and he couldn't afford to be distracted. Better that she be pissed off at him than dead.

Needing some fresh air to clear his head after hardly

sleeping the night before, Warren opened the door to the sleep porch. Too late he discovered the spot was already taken. Tabitha stood on the far side, her back to him as she lifted something steamy to her lips. The steam curled around her cheek as she turned to look at him, her hair still damp from her morning shower, the red glow dimmed now that it was wet.

"Morning." She recovered faster than him, her voice throaty with sleep.

There was an intimacy in knowing he'd been the last one she'd spoken to the night before and he was the first person she'd talked to that morning. The distinction reminded he should have been more worthy of it. He hadn't even had the guts to share a pillow with her.

Of course she'd made tracks mighty damn fast away from him. What was up with that? He should have followed her, held her, reassured her. She'd revealed some heady stuff about herself and her past battles with body image and the eating disorder. What if he'd made it worse?

"Morning. Did you get much sleep, beautiful?" The espressos—or guilt—had kept him up most of the night.

"It was the best I've slept in a while. Must be the mountain air." She stood bundled in a pink winter jacket with a brown collar, but a long nightgown was visible beneath the hem. The pink-and-white cotton grazed a pair of brown suede slippers. Her damp hair was even longer than usual with the weight of the water pulling the waves straight.

She bore little resemblance to the woman he'd met that first night in a sexy negligee that was practically see-through. Had she brought the heavier night clothes on this trip to ward him off? Or was the choice a more practical nod to their destination in the mountains? God knew he was no less attracted to her. She could be sporting a snowsuit and he'd still be turned on.

"Your hair will freeze if you stay out here much longer." He would have liked to have said something warmer. Kinder. He didn't know why such dumb-ass remarks slipped out of his mouth, but he'd never been much of a ladies' man. Too many years shut up in a police precinct with nothing to play with but bullets.

"I'll go in soon." She sipped her coffee while he watched her lips cup the rim of the mug.

He wanted her again already, no matter that he didn't deserve her.

"Are you leaving for work?" She checked her watch before turning her attention back out the screen to the yard below.

"I hadn't really thought about it." Actually, he had. And he'd decided he had enough personal days to stay with her until the threat had passed.

But now he'd experienced how tough it would be for them to be alone together for days and keep their lives getting any more tangled up than they already were.

"I'll be fine here." She passed her mug to him in a silent offer of caffeine. "I read a little about stalkers online last night while you were securing the house and it suggested that leaving town was one of the safest strategies for dealing with this, just like you told me. We're a long way from Manhattan here."

He accepted the mug, tormenting himself with thoughts of placing his mouth exactly where hers had been on the ceramic rim. He didn't. But he wanted to.

Without question he knew he could talk her into a quickie or maybe even a shared shower, but the more time he spent with her—even if only in the physical sense— the more he found himself thinking about her. Wanting her. How could he protect her to the best of his ability if he was making plans for how to get her naked next time?

"Maybe it would help if I could contribute some time to the case." He would swear on his life they weren't tailed the day before. And he wanted to follow up on some of the names she'd given him for Manny's business associates. "As long as you don't use your cell phone at all and you don't use any sort of credit card or ATM card, there's no way this guy could find you."

"I wouldn't even leave the house." She squeezed sections of her hair in a strange gesture that he thought might be intended to break any ice forming on the strands, but as she worked her way around her head he realized she'd been curling it somehow, since the strands started to spring into waves.

"I could leave Buster. And there is an alarm." The house had far better security than her apartment in the city and, as she pointed out, they'd followed the safest protocol for this type of situation. Probably to the point of overkill, but that need to protect her above and beyond the call of duty wasn't something Warren was prepared to examine.

Hell, he could barely acknowledge it without second-guessing the way he conducted this case.

"I would feel guilty if you didn't go." For a woman who went wild for him last night against the fridge, she damn sure couldn't wait to get rid of him today. "I feel bad enough taking you away from your work and mooching off your generosity to let me stay here."

"No. We both know I twisted your arm to leave the city." And she'd accommodated him against her wishes. Then he'd proceeded to make the situation worse by sleeping with her even though he knew things were getting too serious.

He felt it. She had to feel it. Yet he had no intention of ponying up the level of emotional commitment she deserved.

The thought pissed him off.

"Warren?" Gently, she pried her coffee mug from his hand. "Are you okay?"

No doubt his black mood had registered in his face.

"Fine. Just worried about you staying out in the cold and—hell. I know this is awkward between us." He probably owed her more than some half-cocked excuse. "You're an incredible woman, Tabitha. The hottest female I've ever had the privilege of touching, but if I don't keep my head on straight this week—"

She waited patiently. Quietly.

He dug deep, knowing she deserved a clue to what was going through his head, especially after she shared so much with him the night before.

"This would be a bad time for me to lose focus on this case and I have to confess, you've got the power to make me forget everything else."

Eyes widening, she looked startled and he felt all the more the heel for not having told her that sooner. Somehow he thought she knew.

"Wow." She smiled. "I think I'd like hearing your confessions more often."

"Yeah, well… I'm not a man of words, but you can trust the ones I say are absolutely true."

Nodding, she seemed to accept this, to forgive the things he hadn't been able to tell her. Like the other reasons he couldn't get too close.

"I'd rather be with a man who wrestles with what to say than a man who can spout anything and make it sound pretty. Thank you for that." She toasted him with her mug and took another sip, making him feel like crap for not revealing the rest of the absolute truth.

Hell.

Time to get to work. He gestured toward the door to her room—a different door than the one he would use for an exit.

"Good. Excellent, actually. If we're all clear on that point, why don't you head in and I'll see you tonight? I can make the drive in less than two hours so I should be back by eight."

At which time he would damn well keep his hands off her—at least until he was ready to offer her the rest of his reasons for holding back. The deepest truth of all was that he was scared as shit of relationships.

"I'll look forward to it." Her eyes lit from within and her mouth curved into a sexy smile.

Heat rushed over his skin at just that small reminder

of being with her and the subtle hint that she wouldn't mind a repeat performance. Didn't she recognize how far he fell short of treating her the way she deserved to be treated?

"I'll probably work tonight so we can close this case and get you back home."

He'd set better boundaries this time. And while it would be damn hard to resist the allure of Tabitha Everhart under normal circumstances, Warren had the benefit of an incredibly screwed-up past to keep him at bay. All he had to do was think about how much serving time as a teenager had changed him and how much a decade of abuse before that had robbed him of the ability to forge meaningful relationships.

"If you want to work, that's fine with me." She squared her shoulders and headed toward the door to her room, her breath leaving a trail of puffy steam in her wake. "Just don't use it as an excuse to avoid me. I haven't given you any reason to think I expect any more from you than a wild ride, Detective. And after the marriage from hell that I had, believe me, I don't want any warm and fuzzy heart-to-heart chats after our refrigerator encounters, either. But if you'd like to join me tonight in the kitchen for strictly recreational purposes, then I can't wait."

She stalked away from him with a hip-swishing strut guaranteed to turn any man's head and Warren could almost swear he felt a pang of regret in the region of his heart. Hard to believe after how much crap he'd waded through over the last fifteen years without involving much emotion.

And wouldn't it be a hell of a note if he'd been so fired up to protect her from him when maybe it was *him* who was in danger of getting trounced by her?

He didn't really believe it, but damned if the thought didn't call up a rueful smile. He couldn't meet Tabitha for any more midnight sex sessions, but after nightfall he knew that's exactly what he'd be fantasizing about.

Until then, he had a killer to catch so that Tabitha didn't have to think about stalkers and murderers anymore. She'd be able to focus on how to keep herself safe from another kind of predator.

Him.

12

TABITHA RODE THE HIGH of her chutzpah for almost six hours.

She'd been direct and honest with Warren, speaking her mind in a way that felt freeing and healthy. The knowledge that she'd been bold propelled her through the morning while she researched some ideas she'd had for a documentary about the high cost of divorce on society—emotionally and financially. But she'd hit the wall a few hours ago when the realization set in that she was alone and isolated in the mountains and there wasn't anyone she could call to confide in even if Warren hadn't told her to stay off her phone.

Tabitha flipped through the address book she kept in her purse at about seven o'clock while she polished off a prepackaged salad Warren had bought at the local deli counter the day before. She turned the last pages quickly, knowing damn well she wouldn't find anyone in the W-Z section but glancing through anyway. There was no one to call to commiserate with about being imprisoned in this beautiful house since her old friends were all in the business and she didn't want them to think she was trying to draw them into the drama of her divorce.

Although, damn it, that had been a whole year ago.

Shoving aside the plastic container her meal came in, she readjusted her feet against Buster's back where he lay curled up by her chair. What was she gaining by being so considerate of everyone else's feelings when hers had been raked over the coals? Maybe her so-called friends were waiting for her to make the first move since she'd effectively fallen off the face of the earth after realizing she couldn't get a legitimate acting job ten months ago.

Determined to confront some of those old contacts to see where she stood within the small acting community, she picked up Warren's phone to make a few calls. Then set it back down.

If one of Manny's friends or associates—or even Manny himself—was the person stalking her, she shouldn't contact anyone from her old life. Even if she did forego the cell phone to use the safer land-based connection that wasn't listed in her name.

The doorbell rang while she debated making a list of friends to phone next week. Buster barked, immediately alert, although it seemed strange the animal hadn't warned her of the newcomer's approach.

Panic surged through her veins and she froze, waiting to discover what the evening visitor would do. Had they seen her through the curtains even though the blinds were pulled? Certainly the house looked occupied with so many lights on inside. Did Warren have friends nearby who would stop in?

She didn't see any vehicle headlights through the window. Buster's barking increased in volume, the hair around his ruff standing straight up as he sneered a dog warning through the door. Tabitha didn't hear any footsteps walk away or any sounds of the visitor retreating, but after five minutes, Buster had settled down enough to sit by Tabitha's chair again so she assumed anyone who'd been out there was long gone.

Probably the visitor was just a neighbor and she was getting spooked for nothing. Still, Tabitha moved to a window overlooking the front step to make sure all was quiet. It seemed funny to have someone ring the bell this far out in the countryside when she'd never heard a car approach.

The porch lit half the front yard while a lamppost near the driveway illuminated most of the rest. Whoever had rung the bell obviously hadn't minded being seen. And—even more soothing to her worried mind—a plain brown package now rested on the front mat where none had been before.

Relieved the visitor had just been a late delivery, Tabitha opened the door to pull the box inside. Only when she picked up the feather-light package did she realize the brown wrap lacked a label. If the box had been heavier she could have convinced herself a thoughtful neighbor had dropped off cookies or a pie to the local bachelor. Instead, Tabitha reached for the landline to call a phone number Warren had given her that very first night they met.

She didn't miss the irony that the one man who was

wary of getting close to her was the only person she could call right now.

"YOU DIDN'T OPEN IT YET, did you?" Warren charged into the house, grateful to finally get home after Tabitha's call to the precinct. He'd debated taking an undercover car with a light to put in the window, but settled for speeding in his own vehicle the whole way instead.

"No. You said I shouldn't." She still sat in a living room chair, feet tucked under her while reading a book as if the son of a bitch following her all over the state was no big deal.

Memories of his mother's unnatural calm after his father's death floated through his consciousness. She'd been quietly seething underneath, something Warren hadn't seen until later.

But no. That wasn't the case with Tabitha. He could gauge her emotions better as he reached the foot of her chair and saw the way she dog-eared a corner of her page back and forth, back and forth. He'd bet she had been reading the same page of that book for the last hour.

"I shouldn't have left." He'd let his libido cloud his judgment and screwed up by going to work today and God only knew what key information he might have caught if he'd been here today instead of in the city.

"Did you find out anything?"

"A couple of Manny's associates could fit the stalker profile." The news that her ex's name kept turning up in association with both the murder and the underage porn films could keep until he inspected the package.

"But nothing definite?"

"Not yet." He pulled on a pair of gloves to protect the evidence. "Let's take this out in the kitchen first and see if we're freaking out over nothing or if our guy has something new to say."

She nodded, tossing her book into the chair as she stood. Buster stood, too, as if wise to the fact that Tabitha was his charge for the week. The mixed breed was a damn good dog, proof that a creature could be abused within an inch of its life and still turn out honorable. Strong.

Jesus, how could he identify with a dog more than anyone from his own species?

"I don't understand how anybody could have found me." Tabitha's voice sounded far away even though she walked right next to him as he dumped the lightweight box onto the kitchen island beneath an overhead light.

"Maybe he hasn't found you." He still held out some small hope that the unmarked package was someone delivering a personal item to the wrong address or some other kind of mix-up. "But if he has found you, I have an idea how he did it."

"Assuming it's a he."

"Stalking is a predominantly male crime. Women might follow a former lover to do property damage or to have a confrontation, but by and large, the huntlike quality of the crime is something that appeals to men."

"Huntlike?" Her skin appeared unnaturally pale under the harsh task lighting.

"Sorry for the vivid picture, but that's the bottom line

here. Somebody wants to scare the hell out of you first, but once that's done, I think our guy wants you out of the way." De Milo's death suggested their suspect didn't play around.

The thought churned protectiveness in him every bit as fierce as her stalker's hunting mentality. Warren's ability to visit the dark side had given him an edge as a cop and he'd gladly go there again to keep Tabitha safe. His awareness of her was keen even now as she waited, body tense, beside him.

Knife slashing through the tape on the brown paper wrapping, Warren exposed a crisp new postal box. He worked carefully to open it, knowing forensics would inspect every inch of the package to find any hint of their perp.

"I don't understand why. I've taken pains not to make enemies this year. I've busted my ass to be no trouble, not calling friends, not auditioning for parts that I won't get—"

She stopped abruptly, prompting him to turn and look at her before he opened the box. She bit her lip so hard he knew she fought to hold back something more. Emotions? Or did she hide secrets she wasn't willing to share?

He regretted that he wasn't the kind of man she felt she could take into confidence.

"It's not fair." He couldn't touch her without the possibility of contaminating evidence now that he had his gloves on.

"No one said life would be, but I guess you hope—"

She waved away the thought, focusing on the box. "So what's inside?"

He slipped the tab out of the slot and opened the package to find an envelope. Not good stationery, just a run-of-the-mill legal-size envelope with the kind of seal that looked like it came pre-glued. No DNA evidence for this guy, although Warren would have it tested anyhow.

His hope that this package could have reached Tabitha by mistake diminished as he noted the careful attention to making the box as inconspicuous as possible. He used his knife to slice open the envelope, holding the piece over the bag that he'd send to forensics just in case a hair fell out or who knew what.

"Looks like a letter." He unfolded the paper—generic copier style—and read the short, typed missive.

The more you talk to your boyfriend, the faster I'll come for you. Sleep well, Ms. Everhart.
Yours, Red.

She sank into a seat at the island, a high bar stool that caught her before she dropped too far.

"What the hell does that mean?" Her hoarse whisper seemed to speak his thoughts aloud, her soft perfume reminding him of her vulnerability. "And how did the bastard find me?"

"I've got an idea about that." He stashed the evidence in airtight containers but left his gloves on for another kind of search. "I talked it over with some of the detectives at the precinct and the best we came up with was a tracking device."

"As in an electronic thing?"

"Exactly. The technology is readily accessible with the popularity of cars that have Global Positioning Satellite capabilities. Some cell phones come equipped with the same tracking technology so parents can tell where their kids are calling from or spouses can check on each other's whereabouts."

"You're saying someone rigged my phone?" Her breath came in short gasps, her chest rising and falling rapidly in a way that shouldn't draw his eye but did anyway.

"Not necessarily. There's a better chance our guy dropped a device in your suitcase when he broke into your apartment to post the newspaper clippings. If he's been watching you a lot, he might have known which bag you were apt to take if you opted to leave town." He didn't spell out that if the guy stalking her was her ex, he probably knew damn well which items she'd bring with her if she tried taking a trip.

Nodding, she rose to her feet.

"What should we search for?"

"No offense, but I'd rather you let me do the searching. I can bring fresh eyes to your belongings while you might overlook items that are more familiar to you."

Her mouth twisted into a small frown before she agreed.

"Okay."

Setting aside the package, he started toward the stairs to her room.

"Warren?"

172 Just One Look

He hadn't realized she wasn't coming with him. Pivoting on his heel, he watched her twist a strand of hair around one finger for a moment before releasing it. She straightened.

"You don't think he could be listening somehow, do you?" Her tongue swiped over her lower lip. "How do you think he would know if I talked to you?"

The stalker had suggested the more Tabitha confided in him, the sooner he'd hurt her. And wouldn't that do a hell of a lot to help his already stilted relationship with her? Bad enough he felt as if he shouldn't pour out his guts to her, but now the guy on her tail was trying to make her think that she shouldn't talk to Warren, either.

"I'll keep an eye out for listening devices, but I don't think our perp can hear your conversations or else he would have referenced something specific to wig you out even more. He obviously gets off on letting you know how freaking clever he thinks he is."

He could tell she didn't totally buy it. The follower had her scared and Warren couldn't blame her. Warren needed to distract her or reassure her somehow and he wasn't quite sure how to do either. Unless...

Shit. Unless he gave in and started the conversations he didn't want to have. But what right did he have to be selfish when her life might be on the line? It wouldn't help her cause if she sat around and worried herself into a dark place about this guy. He needed her alert and informed, ready to react if the watcher showed up again. And if that meant sidelining her worries with a few stories from his past, he'd do it because damn it, he owed her that much. Especially after the way he'd checked out on her this morning.

This creep was bound to start making mistakes with all the activity in the past two days and Warren would be right there—in the house with her every second—to make sure he caught the bastard when it happened.

THE SENSE OF BEING ALONE had eased tremendously when Warren walked through the door two hours ago, but Tabitha was uncomfortably aware of the heated exchanges that had gone on between them earlier that day. They'd reached a standoff of sorts when she suggested she'd be ready for another sex-with-no-strings encounter in the kitchen tonight and now they were forced to deal with one another on a more business-oriented level.

If you could call her getting stalked *business*. It was for him maybe, but it wasn't the type of pastime she cared for.

She watched him now as he sifted through her possessions. He'd strewn everything out on the bed from her suitcase and went through each item one by one. The empty suitcase was next. He'd saved the purse for last since it had been with her all the time, unlike her suitcase, which had been in her apartment when the sicko who was following her broke in.

"Actually," she spoke up from her spot on a white pine bench at the foot of the bed, "my purse would have been out of my sight while I was on camera the other day."

She didn't think anyone from her work would try to follow her, but then again, Warren thought the link between John de Milo's murder and her might be something film-related.

"You also ran into your ex and the girlfriend who might have reason to be bitter about you." He set down a cosmetic case that contained an embarrassingly large assortment of creams and serums for her skin. "Let's see."

He gestured for her to hand him the bag and she retrieved it from where she'd stuck it under the foot of the bed. Passing him the heavy brown purse, she ignored the implication that her ex could be the one threatening to hurt her. She'd already tried to explain about Manny's methods for making her suffer, but she understood Warren needed to explore every avenue.

That doggedness—or was it cynicism?—made him good at his job.

"What made you become a cop?" She tried not to wince as he dumped everything from inside her purse onto the bed. Stray coins rolled into lipstick cases and pens while a few loose pieces of paper—receipts for small purchases—floated more slowly to the chenille spread.

When he didn't immediately start digging through the contents, Tabitha realized her question was apparently another one of his hot buttons since his hand stalled in midair, half crumpling the leather-and-canvas satchel.

"Never mind." She retracted the question with a wave of her hand. "We could always discuss the weather. Or your favorite shade of my lipstick from the five tubes I seem to have collected in the bottomless depths of my handbag."

She reached for one of the tubes, not remembering

the shade in the silver case and wondering if one of the makeup people had slipped her a bonus sample.

"The cops investigating my father's murder screwed me over with a crap interpretation of the ballistics evidence. For months, they thought I was the killer."

His detached words stunned her. The lipstick fell out of her hand as her gaze shot to his face.

His expression remained blank. Emotionless. Except for a slow tic beneath one eye that gave him away. Even so, everything else about him gave off a "stand the hell back" vibe she recognized well enough. It pained him to talk about this and somehow any physical comfort she might offer would only make the pain worse.

"I'm so sorry." The simple soft words didn't come close to covering what she felt, what she wanted to offer him, but they would have to suffice because she could see that right now he wouldn't accept any more from her. She didn't know, however, if she was sorrier for asking or that the police had made an error that had hurt the family.

Although she knew there was far more to this story, she also guessed he wasn't the kind of guy to share it. Especially not with a woman he wanted to distance himself from. Yet for some reason he'd decided to tell her tonight and damned if she wouldn't do her best to put aside her own problems and be here for him. She sensed the best way to help would be to simply listen and let him do the telling at his own pace. No pushing or babbling from her.

Slowly, his bloodless fists unclenched, the color returning to his knuckles.

"The truth came out eventually, thanks to a cop who resorted to more old-school tactics to prompt a second ballistics test." He exhaled, obviously reaching deep for the words. He rubbed his hands together between his knees, staring at the ground. His hands eased to a stop.

He frowned as he reached for the lipstick tube she'd dropped.

"What's this?"

Tabitha struggled to keep up with the abrupt shift in the conversation. She was still stuck back there in the world where Warren had been unjustly accused of killing his own father and now they were swapping to a discussion about cosmetics?

She squinted to see the label on the bottom and then realized neither end of the thin silver cylinder had a label. One end looked like clear black plastic, the kind of dark window situated on the end of a remote control.

"It's not another lipstick?" She could see the seam in the middle that separated the top from the rest of the tube, but when he twisted the two ends apart, no Raspberry Rouge or Pink Paradise color appeared.

A red light blinked on a thin wand inside the case, the way a car alarm flashed when it was armed.

When Warren didn't explain the device's significance, Tabitha started to ask about it.

"Ohmigod. Do you think—"

His hand gently covered her mouth as he dropped the device to the bed again. The scent of his skin had an immediate, soothing effect on her even though it scared her to death to think someone wanted to keep tabs on her this badly.

Warren moved close to her to whisper in her ear through the veil of her hair.

"Let's be discreet just in case it operates as a listening device. Okay?"

She nodded, mute with new fears for her safety. For his. They'd unwittingly led a dangerous enemy right to Warren's doorstep.

13

WARREN WEIGHED their options later that night as he watched Tabitha sleeping on his couch in the hours before dawn. Should they stay or should they leave?

From his seat on the floor beside the couch, Warren's gaze fell on a strand of hair that drooped over her cheek and fell under her nose as she lay curled on her side, knees tucked close to her chest. The wavy red lock moved in time with her breathing, flying out over her soft lips when she exhaled, then falling limp along her skin when she inhaled.

He could watch her forever. Content to keep his hands to himself as long as he could ensure her safety since that's what mattered most right now. He needed to protect her.

The clock ticked quietly on the wall behind her, reminding him he had to figure out a game plan fast. He'd already had a couple of off-duty friends make the drive up to the Catskills to retrieve the GPS tracking device. They'd met at a gas station a few blocks away and Warren had the officers take his car back to Manhattan along with the GPS device to mislead their perp. Anyone watching the place would think Warren and Tabitha had ditched the country house since Warren had left in the car and walked home along the river under cover of dark.

Warren would repay his friends with their choice of weeks at the Catskills house next fall and with any luck, the stalker would track his car back into the city, far away from here. In the meantime, they were staying in the house with no lights on and limiting Buster's outdoor time as a precaution.

Leaving Warren to do what? He'd added a few security measures to the property before his 1:00 a.m. run to the gas station, increasing the sensitivity of motion detectors so that the whole place would shriek with alarms and light if so much as a squirrel ventured onto the lawn. What more could he do to keep her safe besides move her somewhere else?

He reached over Tabitha to brush the hair from her face, smoothing the strands into place as he considered the dilemma. Move Tabitha to another location that might ward off the stalker longer but would be less familiar home terrain to defend? Or keep her here, a location the perp knew about, and risk a confrontation sooner but keep the advantage of home court where Warren had more tricks in his bag?

The first option might be safer in the short term, but how long could she hide from an enemy who obviously knew her and her habits well? Tabitha might be better off risking a quicker confrontation to win back her life and her privacy sooner.

Even if it meant Warren would have to say goodbye that much earlier.

"What are you thinking?" Tabitha's voice surprised him and he wondered how long she'd been awake.

Had she felt the longing in his touch?

"I'm trying to figure out how to say your ex's live-in girlfriend has been making phone calls to fellow producers to make sure they don't hire you." He hadn't really been thinking about that, but he couldn't tell her what else had been going through his head—the desire for her that wasn't going to be quenched by a few shared nights in his bed.

He'd been so close to telling her everything about his past before they'd found that tracking device. Now, he didn't know how to get back to it. Telling her as much as he had pained him enough. He'd get back to it soon though, and it would either scare her off for good or—

He couldn't allow himself to think about the alternative since the possibility might rouse hopes he didn't dare think about yet.

"Evelyn?" Tabitha blinked once before her eyebrows shot higher. "How do you know?"

"I made a few phone calls today from the precinct and some of your ex's colleagues were extremely cooperative since they seem to take John de Milo's death very seriously. The New York film industry might be a close-knit group, but they're apparently more willing to crack when one of their own gets whacked."

"And one of these people told you Evelyn has been making calls about me?"

Sitting up, she seemed to shake off her sleepiness, her eyes growing more alert. Still, a line from the pillow seam creased her cheek, reminding him she should be sleeping instead of worrying about an enemy who wouldn't hesitate to use lethal force.

"I heard the same thing from more than one person. It speaks of a vindictiveness that could be in line with the stalking crime." And if that was the case, Evelyn would pay dearly for what she'd done to Tabitha. Hours after Warren had arrived home his heart still hadn't stopped racing from fears for what could have happened to this woman while he'd been gone.

Hell, his mind hadn't stopped spinning every conceivable scenario, either, filling his head with all the ways someone could have gotten to her in his absence.

"Even though most stalkers aren't female," she pointed out. "And I can't imagine what she'd have against de Milo."

Struggling to shake off the dark images that threatened to swallow him, Warren wanted to touch her, to taste her, to feel her on a physical level and chase away the mental crap.

For a split second he imagined what it would be like to tell her that, to unburden himself for a moment. But the last time he'd shared his nightmarish imaginings with someone—his mother—she'd written them off as demented proof that he should have stayed in juvie instead of letting the cops pin the murder on her older, favored son.

The way her words cut to his very soul had given him all the impetus he needed to keep his mouth shut where his past was concerned. He redirected his thoughts to Tabitha's situation.

"Donata thinks the killer was afraid de Milo knew something about the distribution of underage porn, remember? Do you think Evelyn could have ties to that industry?" He didn't want to lead her toward any preconceived conclusions so he didn't get specific.

"She does hang around with a lot of younger girls." She sat up on the couch, dragging a blue blanket with her that she must have snagged out of his linen closet. "I just assumed she liked to have a few wanna-be actresses at her beck and call to play suck-up to her and pick up her dry cleaning. But maybe there's more to it?"

Warren nodded even though he didn't quite buy the idea of Evelyn as Tabitha's stalker, either. He rose from the floor to sit next to her on the couch.

"The porn industry isn't exactly full of female executives, either, so there are two counts against Evelyn being our stalker." The weight of his body on the couch made the cushion angle downward, the movement tipping Tabitha's body onto a subtle incline toward him. "Maybe she likes to buck convention when it comes to gender stereotypes."

"Are you kidding? Have you seen the rack on this woman? Everything about her shouts stereotype. She's a home-wrecking, boob-lifting, man-chasing, rump-shaking cheat who has been trading in one man for another ever since she was old enough to date. Manny was such a big ticket for her she dropped her attorney boyfriend like a bad habit when she saw how much my husband could help her career."

"An attorney?"

"Manny's former attorney was Evelyn's previous live-in." She tucked her blanket around her feet, her hair slithering off her shoulder to fall on his as she leaned forward. "Manny managed to stay friends with the guy for some months afterward but I guess they recently parted ways. Braeden was nothing like Evelyn, though. A grounded guy who took care of business rather than just talking about it."

"Any chance he's tied to underage porn?" Warren suspected that connection would be the key to finding the killer, but it was an area he hadn't investigated much yet. He'd been so concerned with protecting Tabitha he hadn't looked too far past her link to the killer.

"He's the last person I'd suspect, but what do I know? He's an ambitious Texas lawyer who came to New York to make his mark and he's worked his butt off to do that, including kissing Manny's ass and forking over his girlfriend when Manny wanted her, too."

That sounded more in line with a typical stalker profile. Someone marginalized. Someone who wanted revenge after stuffing down the need for a long time.

"Any reason he'd call himself—" He stopped himself midsentence. "His name's O'Leary, right? An Irish guy?" Warren had spent less time researching the attorney because his ties to filmmaking weren't as obvious as most of Manny's other colleagues and the screen name the stalker had chosen for the original e-mail he'd sent Tabitha was "first take."

"He's Irish. But he's got dark hair and blue eyes."

Warren nodded. "I'll have him checked out. In the

meantime, I put somebody on your ex-husband at all times. As of midnight, he was still in Manhattan."

"I appreciate what you're doing for me." The warmth of her at his side brought him a kind of pleasure beyond sexual interest.

He stretched his arm around her automatically, before he remembered he needed to draw boundaries to keep his head above water around her.

"What do you think of staying here?" He asked the question from out of the blue, needing to make arrangements soon if she wanted to leave. "We might be safer in the short term if we leave now since our guy has tracked this place already. But sending the tracking device back to Manhattan will buy us a little time and at least up here we're prepared." He'd already made up his mind about what he wanted to do, but it didn't seem fair to make the call without consulting her.

"In spite of everything, I feel safe here." She shrugged as if to acknowledge that made no sense. Her V-necked T-shirt slipped a little sideways with the gesture and he could see a pink lace bra strap hugging her shoulder.

"I don't know how long we might be here before he—or she—makes a return appearance." He tried not to be distracted by that hint of pink clinging to her pale skin and it was all he could do not to lift his hand a few inches up her forearm to cover that exposed flesh.

"You're saying we might be stuck together up here for a little while?" Her mock-innocent expression reminded him she had a sense of humor despite the crappy turn her luck had taken this week.

He wondered what kind of effect she might have on him if he'd met her before life had hurt her. Would her smile at full-wattage have brought him to his knees? Or would he have overlooked a woman who didn't understand about the scars life could leave?

"I'm saying we've got to stick close until we have your stalker in custody and we're a hundred percent sure it's the right guy." The idea of being close to her for such damn dangerous reasons shouldn't turn him on. But it did. "Is that going to be a problem for you?"

"No problem here. How about you?" Her finger hooked in the neckline of her T-shirt before she tugged it gently back in place. And although it covered her shoulder again, there had been a moment where the fabric gapped away from her chest and gave him a quick glimpse of spectacular cleavage.

She threatened his sanity because she made him feel too much. Passion. Protectiveness. Caring. Once he started feeling those things fully his whole mechanism for dealing with his past would explode in his face. He couldn't simultaneously feel the things she inspired and close off the painful crap from the old days, too. Something had to give.

"There are going to be problems." He knew it without question. The more time they spent together, the less he could pretend they were just having simple, recreational sex. "But I don't think either one of us is going to find it in ourselves to care."

He reached to pull her across his body and on top of him, his whole body straining closer to her scent, her softness, her taste. He wouldn't deny himself what he wanted more than anything.

Tabitha followed the dictate of his arms around her, letting Warren lift and reposition her on the wide slab of coffee table across from him so they were face-to-face. His lips were hot on hers, dominating the kiss with fire and insistence instead of tenderness. She saw the kiss for what it was, sexual need fired by thwarted good intentions, and she wanted it anyway.

A wildness lurked in Warren that surfaced every time they kissed and she found herself seeking it out time and time again. She wanted the kisses and the heat, yes. But she wanted to uncover the private man full of dark secrets and anguish she couldn't understand.

Sex put her in touch with that man.

Her fingers grasped ineffectually at his shirt hem, her hands incapable of making progress when his kisses consumed her. His hands smoothing down her sides, he cupped her breasts and spanned her ribs with his fingers. She arched against him, a whimper escaping from her throat as she fell into him. Her T-shirt provided little barrier to his touch, yet he skimmed it off her body in one fluid motion.

He delved deeper into her mouth as his kisses turned more deliciously aggressive. The wicked intent she sensed behind that wet mating of mouths thrilled her on a primal level, stripping away the need for anything more than sweaty, intense sex to leave them both gasping for breath.

She tugged at his shirt again, needing to feel his body

against hers. Hot, naked muscles against her aching skin. With fumbling touches, nerves buzzing with anticipation and need, she finally pulled the material off him, breaking their kiss long enough to accomplish the deed.

They stared at one another for a moment, the sound of ragged breathing filled her ears. His. Hers. The soft pants mingled between them. He held her away from him as his gaze swept her whole body.

"Wait. I want to look at you." He seemed fascinated with the lace on her bra strap, running his finger underneath the thin strip of material without venturing deeper into the cups, where she wanted his touch all the more.

"I want to see you, too." She reached for his belt, ready to strip away the rest of his clothes faster than she'd ditched his shirt, but he imprisoned her wrist.

"I'm running the show tonight." His hold didn't hurt her, but the grip didn't allow her to move, either. "I'm skating on thin ground right now."

He didn't explain that, but she sensed it had something to do with whatever he held back from her, whatever dark secrets lurked inside him.

"Okay. Just don't make me wait too long." Her breath came fast as she waited for him to release her. His slow perusal of her in the shadowed light from the hallway made her feel hot. Sexy. Wet.

"I make no promises." He flicked the bra strap off her shoulder with one careless flip of his finger. His other hand still held her fast.

A pleasurable shiver trembled through her, tingling over her skin and stirring the heat between her thighs.

"Please." She moistened her lips with a sweep of her tongue, willing to resort to whatever tactics necessary to get his hands all over her again. His mouth, too. Her whole body trembled in wary alertness for his next move. His next touch.

"I'll please you, all right." The edge to his voice mirrored the firm grip of his hands, the unapologetic scrutiny of her body as he unfastened her jeans. "As long as you understand this is all I can give you."

"That's all I need." She swayed toward him, dizzy with his scent. His taste lingering in her mouth. "You don't seem to recognize that this is so much more than I've had in a long time."

His arm snaked around her shoulders to gently clench her hair in his fist. He held her there, staring at her, knowing her most intimate secrets when she understood so little about him.

Then his mouth landed on hers again and she forgot to think. Breathe. Do anything but cling to him and let those kisses drug her. Her scalp tingled and tightened as he released her hair to run his hands down her back. He pulled her off the table and into his lap, her legs tangling with his until he resituated her crosswise, her limbs draped over the couch while he cupped her bottom to his groin. Hands curved around her buttocks through her open jeans before he skimmed the denim farther down her hips.

Heat burned away everything but the promise of fulfillment he could bring her. He might shut her out of his head and his heart, but his body was all hers for tonight and she knew that meant more than he would admit. Sex would be their meeting ground, their entrée to something deeper they couldn't avoid.

And if she was wrong, she'd take away scorching memories to keep her warm if Warren walked out of her life as quickly as he'd burst into it.

14

WARREN CAREENED HEADLONG into a kind of sexual unconsciousness, a realm where it was easy to forget everything else. At least until tomorrow.

She poured over him like honey, her skin hot and sweet as he tasted her neck, her throat. Her rump shifted in his lap, incinerating any reserve with his ability to hold back. He gathered her up in his arms and squeezed her closer, increasing the pressure of her hip against him.

The movement incited something in her, wresting a cry from her throat as she rubbed her breasts over his chest and broke his kiss to nip his shoulder as she wrestled his belt out of his pants. He freed the hooks on her bra and slid the pink lace off so he could feel her without impediment.

The warm silk of her skin fried his brain cells, robbing him of any thought save having her. All of her.

His fingers abandoned their mission of touching her in an effort to remove the rest of her clothes. The soft, mewling sounds she made in the back of her throat didn't help since he knew she craved his touch as much as he wanted to give it to her.

Her eyes went wide as he lifted her off the couch all together, skimming the denim from her endless legs and taking a bogus scrap of pink that she must pass off as panties from her hips. Tabitha naked was a sight that would fill any red-blooded male with reverence and oh, man, he was feeling mighty damn grateful for the view right about now. His twill pants didn't come off as quickly as her clothes, but who could work fast with a zipper embedded in his skin?

When they were both naked he covered her, pinning her to the sofa with his body, his legs spreading hers. This was what he wanted, what he'd tried like hell to deny, what he'd want tomorrow even more fiercely for having indulged himself today. The woman could tempt him.

He yanked his gaze up to her eyes to find her staring at him with equal intensity, soul bared for his viewing. He should look away. Focus on the sex. But some sort of communication happened without his permission or his foreknowledge, an understanding that surpassed mutual orgasms or any kind of cosmic sex encounter. He closed his eyes to shut it out, knowing he was too late.

Sheathing himself in the condom she'd produced from somewhere, Warren refused to let it rattle him. He lowered his mouth to her breast and drew on the taut nipple, savoring the taste of her on his tongue. She wriggled and writhed and guided his hand between her legs, directing his fingers to her sex. Inviting him inside.

He held back, touching her only with his forefinger, circling around that most heated of places. She stirred beneath him, arching up to meet him, to open herself. And ah, hell, but it took willpower to wait.

Reaching up to her mouth, he slid one finger between her teeth, allowing her to draw on the digit. The slick soft feel of her around him brought an answering throb in his cock, as if her mouth worked directly on his shaft. Sliding his finger away, he carried the dampness south to mingle with the heat between her legs.

Tracing the slick seam he played with her, fondled her, plucked her sex until her breath caught and held, eyes rolling back before her lids fluttered closed. She was so near the edge her whole body thrummed with the tension of it, heart hammering her chest and his with the want of release.

Only then did he ease a finger inside her, first one and then two. He reached deep, stretching, massaging her clit with his thumb.

Her head twisted from side to side, finally burying in the couch cushion behind her as he worked his way in as deeply as he could go. Bending to kiss her, he caught her moan as she unwound for him with one shuddering cry after another. Her nails raked his shoulders, his forearms, as she held on, hips twisting against the pleasure.

His body hummed with one kind of satisfaction while he waited to find another. Edging back he stared down at her, cheeks flushed, nipples tinged with color. She was an incredible sight. Her lips were plump and wet, her panting breaths warm on his chest as her cries turned to occasional gasps while residual spasms eased.

She reached for his shoulder, splaying a hand across his chest as if she would continue where they left off.

"Not so fast." Tilting away from her, he gathered her up in his arms and lifted them. He sat on the couch and had her straddle him, her thighs spilling over his so she was positioned right where he wanted her. "I'm not nearly done with you yet."

A fleeting smile danced over her mouth, eyes glittering with satisfaction.

"If I had my way, you wouldn't be done for a very long time." She made a show of sucking on her finger and then circled the tip of his cock with it, playing on the way he'd teased her earlier.

Gripping her hips, he lifted her, savoring the feel of feminine flesh as he pushed his way inside. The floral scent of her skin rose from her neck and shoulders to intoxicate him. He inhaled deeply.

Her eyes widened as he seated himself all the way inside, red hair cloaking her in a fiery contrast to her pale skin as she fell against him. The sweetness of that gesture, the trust implicit in her total submission stirred something deep within him. Unexpected tenderness threatened to level him as she wound her arms around him, holding on to him as if she wouldn't ever let go.

He didn't want to acknowledge the sudden connection he felt to Tabitha that went far beyond duty, but it seemed to suddenly be there as naturally as his next breath.

He gripped her thighs, withdrawing from her slightly and then burying himself inside her all over again, hoping he could find a rhythm of mind-blowing monkey sex that would make him forget all about this...bond he felt for her.

In a state of frenzy he palmed her deliciously curved ass and worked her hips to accommodate a faster pace, willing her to understand his need to forget. To lose himself in this.

But she only kissed him and teased him, swiveling her hips in a move that would make a pole-dancing stripper proud. The blatant carnality of the act should have dislodged the tenderness he felt. But instead the massive sexual windup only seemed to fuel his sense that something was right between them.

When he couldn't hold on any longer he tipped his head to hers and release came in one butt-kicking moment after another in an endless chain of spasms.

Holy hell.

He couldn't think, talk or take a deep breath. He felt more wasted than when he'd swam in an Ironman competition two years ago in a need to move on after his divorce.

The swimming and running and biking had made it easy to forget about Melinda. But having amazing sex with Tabitha had been counterproductive to say the least. Because right now, he only wanted her more than ever.

Maybe the time had come to quit running and simply share a small piece of himself. Not just any piece. But the one that would scare off Tabitha the quickest, because God knew he wasn't doing a very good job of staying away when left to his own devices.

How could a man slip away when you were holding him so tight?

Tabitha loosened her hold on Warren even though she didn't want to. She'd pushed for this closeness and she would not make him regret it. Not after he'd given her so much pleasure her body could barely contain it all. Her whole being sang with the thrill of fulfillment he brought.

"I never finished telling you about the ballistics screwup." His words shocked her as they sat together face-to-face in the dark.

Buster paced the nearby kitchen in his makeshift pen, his nails ticking along the linoleum with each step. The clock chimed softly in the hallway in the silence that followed while she gulped down her surprise.

"I didn't know how much you were prepared to tell me." She knew how tough it had been to share her shortcomings. Her past. She couldn't imagine how hard it must be for a detective to trot out his past as a wrongly accused killer when the victim had been an abusive father.

What a nightmare of a household he must have been raised in. Chills raced over her skin that didn't have anything to do with the drafts in the old house. She wrapped her arms around him to share warmth and comfort.

"In all honesty, I was relieved that I got a reprieve because it's still rough for me to revisit that time." He lifted her off him to sit next to him on the couch, then he tugged the fleece blanket over them.

Now she ducked into the fleece all over again, amazed how much warmer it felt now that she had someone to share the cover with.

"You didn't connect the pieces for me, but since you told me before that your brother's prison time is almost up, I gathered that it must have been him who kept silent while you were accused of the crime." She hoped it was okay to tread through those waters, but she thought maybe it would help to give him a jumping-off place. She wanted to make it easier for him. To take away some of the pain that had to come from any memories.

"Oh, yeah. He kept silent all right. I hated him for that when I first found out he'd sold me up the river, but eventually…" He scrubbed a weary hand over his eyes, taking an extra moment to scratch his temple. "He convinced me I'd be better off serving the time as a juvenile since we *had* been abused and since my sentence would be lighter."

The horror of that logic congealed in her chest. What a horrific betrayal to carry around for the rest of his life. How difficult it would be to trust anyone again. She blinked back tears, then decided, what the hell. He deserved every tear burning the backs of her lids.

"What a terrible burden to put on you." Grief stung her heart at the thought of his older brother making such a request. No matter how much the boys resented—hated—their father, asking Warren to falsely admit to a crime was wrong.

"I'll admit it felt like the end of the world at first." He squeezed her shoulder, drawing her into the confidences she suspected he'd been stomping down for days. "But the truth is, my father was out of control, my mother lied to every social services worker who ever looked in to the case, and I might have been dead before I turned eighteen if my brother hadn't—"

He closed his eyes and Tabitha stroked her hand over his chest in a sorry effort to soothe away the hurts.

"He shot your father to save you." She recognized how an eighteen-year-old might see the world that way. And maybe it was true. But it had still been too much to put on a sixteen-year-old's shoulders when there could have been other ways to handle it. Like, say, the eighteen-year-old owning up to what he did, damn it.

Then again, what did she know? Sometimes people who'd been traumatized couldn't see their way through their pain well enough to find a way out.

"He shot my father with the same caliber rifle we kept at our Connecticut house for hunting season. In fact, he'd taken me hunting the same day as the murder and made sure I took a couple of shots."

"So ballistics matched the murder weapon to your hunting rifle?" She remembered him saying that he'd gotten into the field to make sure mix-ups didn't happen.

"Yes. I found out afterward he'd wiped clean the gun that he'd never fired, while mine showed my fingerprints. And I failed the gunpowder test they gave me at the police station." He shook his head. "Between that and the circumstantial evidence, the D.A. found enough to convict. But if someone with a little more field experience had looked at the bullets closely, the ammo fired from my rifle couldn't have killed my father since the firing chamber in the weapon left a distinctive imprint."

She was stunned. Not just at the miscarriage of justice, but that a man who'd been so robbed by the system could embrace law enforcement as a lifetime mission. Even Buster in the next room seem to sense the wretched pain of the past and whimpered from his kitchen pen.

"And your brother never spoke up?" She didn't understand why Warren seemed to write off his sibling's contribution to a murder conviction, but then she knew bonds between family could be complicated.

"He saw my father getting worse more clearly than I could. Andy saw the progression of the beatings—the rage—better than me or my mother, who had grown comfortable in her permanent state of denial."

That was sad for more reasons than she could count. What a horrible, heartbreaking position for both boys.

"Did anyone suspect your brother?" She didn't know how to ask if Warren had ever tried to implicate him. Better to dance around the tough questions, she decided, and see what information rose to the surface. She didn't want to stir up more than he cared to offer.

"The police didn't suspect him because he was out of the house, free of the abuse. But Andy knew with him gone to deflect some of my father's…attention…I'd be dead before I hit eighteen."

"And you went along with him?"

"Not at first." He shifted. Tense. "I didn't put the pieces together to confront him until I was halfway through my stint in juvie when I finally faced up to a truth I probably knew all along. Seeing how hard some of those kids had become made me recognize that brittleness in myself. In my brother."

"So then he confessed to you but asked you to keep quiet about it because his time would be harder than yours." She knew she couldn't possibly comprehend the full extent of family dynamics that came into play there, but it was difficult to find compassion for the man who'd made Warren suffer that way. Something about the way he held himself very still when he said *juvie* told her bad things had happened in that place.

"Being there was an eye-opener, and I didn't exactly have some picture-perfect childhood. There was a move at that time toward more rehabilitative efforts and the net result was giving some bad, bad kids too much free rein to hurt the ones who still had some heart left. After what I'd seen inside those walls, I knew I didn't want my brother in a real prison." His blue eyes glittered with an icy ferocity.

The coldness in that glance might have scared some people, but mostly Tabitha was just scared for him. Whatever he'd seen during his so-called rehabilitative months would likely haunt him for the rest of his life.

Her heart hurt for him and the piece of his soul he'd lost during that time.

"But it wasn't your call to make whether your brother went to prison or not. It's up to the justice system." And she hated it that the system failed him. First by social services not taking the abused children away from a dangerous household and later by misleading evidence.

He picked at a piece of lint on the blanket as some of the tension seeped slowly out of his shoulders.

"Eventually that's what happened. A cop who'd come out on a domestic violence call at our house took an interest in the case and did a second ballistics test that proved the bullet that killed my father couldn't have come from the firing chamber of the hunting rifle. Two weeks after he secured those results, this cop found my brother's rifle that he'd bought illegally."

The wind outside creaked through the house and Tabitha realized the whole world seemed quiet except for the howling gusts—Buster had settled down since his lonesome cries earlier. She took comfort in that quiet now, finding peace in simply sitting with Warren while the world went crazy outside the walls of the graceful old farmhouse.

"So they set you free and cleared your record." She traced a ripple of muscle along the warm sinew of his forearm, somehow knowing in her gut that he hadn't shared the worst of what happened while he was locked up. But she suspected there were some things a person could never share and she'd recognized that boundary when he'd told her the story.

"I hated that detective for putting my brother away when I'd already done time for the crime." He gripped her wandering hand and then lined up their fingers before interlocking them. He stared at the bond he'd created while his thoughts seemed a world away. "I don't know how I went from hate to grudging respect, but that's how it went. In the end you had to admire someone who wouldn't accept a lie. After four years of college and faking like I belonged there, I entered the police academy."

Where he made sure no one else was sent to jail on poorly interpreted evidence. He didn't need to say it for her to understand.

"You became a cop." She turned over that knowledge, looking at it with new eyes. "You made it a mission."

He winced slightly at her word choice.

"I became a cop because it seemed like the right thing to do at the time. But I didn't realize how much pride I took in the badge until I started making some questionable decisions this week."

"Because of me." No wonder he'd been silently pulling away from her. She'd felt it but hadn't been quite sure why.

"No." He shook his head, determination in his eyes and in the squeeze of his grip around her fingers. "Because of me. I was the one who showed up on your doorstep wanting more. But technically I should have waited a few weeks to be sure nothing would develop on your case."

His spin on events didn't take away the fact that she'd been the cause of some regrets for him. And that hurt her whether he wanted it to or not.

"Warren, I—"

"I have the right to a personal life. I'll talk to a review

committee about it, but I can tell you right now that if I had it to do over, I wouldn't change one thing."

The way their palms were sealed together by their fingers seemed like proof of his words, the physical manifestation of a larger connection they shared in spite of everything they'd intended.

A door had opened between them and Tabitha felt all her emotions sucked right through it, irrevocably tied up in him. No matter that she was on the run for her life, she'd found something precious on that journey because meeting Warren made her want to take chances again, to risk herself in spite of all the ways she'd been burned before.

And whether or not Warren wanted anything more with her, she knew she'd never regret gambling with her heart on such an incredible guy.

She searched for the right words to tell him as much, to let him know she didn't want to put any more walls between them. But before she could express a fraction of the emotions pouring through her, the security alarm blared a high-pitched wail as exterior lights flashed on all over the property.

Someone was outside.

15

WARREN HAD NO MEMORY of putting his clothes on, but he must have pulled on his pants during his sprint across the room because they were in place by the time he opened the back door to admit the two local cops standing on the porch.

"Can I help you?" Warren didn't appreciate the arrival and he made a mental note of the badge numbers the younger men flashed under his nose.

His scheme to keep Tabitha in residence on the sly was destined for failure now that anyone watching the house could tell there were still occupants inside. Buster went crazy in the kitchen, the dog's vicious barks reminding Warren that he could attack when the mood struck and now—facing down a couple of local cops—definitely wasn't a good time for Buster to let loose. He'd have to put the dog in the basement.

"We're following up on a tip from a neighbor who said she saw someone *skulking* about. Her word, not ours." The younger officer grinned, ample ears lifting his hat slightly on his head as a toothy smile kicked in. "Any chance you saw a skulker in a white sedan?"

"You think she saw someone near this property?" He stilled, plenty interested in his neighbor's report.

The older officer—by all of a couple of years— stepped forward, his eyes darting around the house behind Warren. No doubt the sounds of a psycho dog were making the guys uneasy.

"She saw the car parked on the road between her house and yours and thought you had company, but then she observed someone walking down by the river in the dark and gave us a call to check it out."

"Maybe you'd better come in. Just let me park the dog downstairs." He figured it couldn't hurt to get the local cops on his side, especially since he could feel Tabitha's nervousness as she lurked in the back hallways of the house. Listening. Worried.

She'd been so nonjudgmental about his past. About his brother. He appreciated the open mind almost as much as he appreciated her not digging through his memories of juvenile detention. Some ghosts were better left in the past.

He didn't know what Tabitha thought about him now that she knew the truth, but at least she'd listened without freaking out the way Melinda had. His ex-wife had nearly lost her mind to discover Warren had served time, even if it had been a mistake. But maybe she'd just been shaken because she could finally understand his commitment to his job that ensured he'd never take that slot in his father's lucrative company.

No, Tabitha definitely wasn't the same kind of woman as Melinda Cartwright, but Warren didn't plan to make another move with Tabitha until he got a better read on her reaction. And right now, she might be too keyed up about her stalker's return to give much thought to a future that might—if he were very fortunate—include Warren.

TABITHA DIDN'T KNOW HOW to contribute to the investigation at this point. She staked out a spot on the sleep porch with Buster as the sun rose that morning, grateful for the chance to get fresh air without having to actually leave the house.

Wrapped in her winter coat and a blanket she'd taken off the end of her bed, she settled for a corner against the wall of the house. Sitting on the floor allowed her to stay below the screened section of the walls, preventing anyone outside from seeing her.

Not that she expected her presence to be a mystery since the police visit last night. Warren had talked to the local cops well into the night, long after she fell asleep. She'd stumbled down the stairs shortly before dawn to find him at the computer, mumbling something about tracking online orders for underage porn to a distribution point. She'd assumed that route would lead him to the stalker but she had no idea how long it might take or how reliable the information would be. If it had been a simple job, no doubt the police would have done it already.

Now she just needed a few minutes to get her head together before she faced Warren again, a little time to figure out how to proceed from here. He'd shown her a part of himself she knew he didn't reveal to many people. Would he regret the intimacy after he'd fought so hard to keep some emotional distance from her?

God knows she'd done some fighting of her own, too. But the hell Manny had put her through seemed more manageable now, maybe because she could see her way out of it. She had a plan for achieving different dreams, for returning to filmmaking the way she'd planned so many years ago.

What would Warren think of her behind the camera?

A cold breeze stung her cheek as the wind whipped across the mountains and Tabitha lifted her face into the bracing air. The day seemed rife with new possibilities if only she knew who wanted to stop her—permanently.

The classical ring tone on her cell phone chimed from underneath the blanket, startling Buster as much as her. She hadn't asked Warren about cell phone use since her stalker had discovered their whereabouts. Was she not supposed to answer it? Or did it matter since a cell couldn't be traced to a particular location?

The caller ID screen showed the name of her ex's law firm. Former law firm now that Manny and Braeden had parted ways. Remembering Warren's questions about Braeden and his connection to Evelyn, Tabitha made a split decision to answer the call.

"Hello?"

"Tabitha, it's Braeden O'Leary. Do you have a minute?"

She looked around the sleep porch at Buster lying contentedly in the corner.

"I guess so. But I thought you weren't representing

Manny anymore?" She'd barely been able to afford her own lawyer in the divorce, and Braeden had made mincemeat out of the guy so Tabitha had every reason to dislike Braeden. But she didn't. She'd always empathized with him that Manny had chosen his attorney's girlfriend for an affair.

Still, Warren told her this guy could fit the profile of a stalker. Of course, so could some of Manny's other business associates, but she would be cautious.

"That's what I wanted to talk to you about. I think it's time you knew a few things about your ex's business dealings now that I'm not on Manny's payroll anymore. Do you have some time to meet today so we could talk about it in private?"

Unease pricked her skin, creeping over her shoulders and up the back of her neck. Could Braeden possess information that would incriminate Manny? Warren had thought all along her ex played a role in the stalking. Did Braeden know something about that? Or did he simply wish to alert her to some of Manny's underhandedness during the divorce proceedings? Either way, the promised information enticed her.

"Today is busy for me," she hedged, unwilling to admit her location. "Could we discuss it now, over the phone?"

She could have Warren listen in with her.

There was a pause on the other end of the call.

"I'm really putting my professional reputation at risk by talking to you. You can't at least offer me some assurance that what I say will go no further? You know how unreliable cell phone connections can be when it comes to privacy." His censorious tone told her she wouldn't be receiving any sensitive information this way.

"Actually, Braeden, I'm out of town for a little while. Some personal problems." That kept things vague enough. "Can I call you back in an hour after I work out some of the details and I'll figure out a time we could talk?"

Warren would know how they could set up a meeting so that she'd be secure. Or maybe he could be with her when she spoke to Braeden. Then again, maybe Braeden would never confide in her if a cop was involved. The complications multiplied.

"Look, Tabitha. In case you haven't figured it out already, your ex is a dangerous man with considerable power. I'm not going to jeopardize my own work in the industry to help you when I'm already sticking my neck out to make this call. Tell me where to meet you and I'll be there, but don't jerk me around. If you're going to try involving your crappy lawyer or anyone else, the deal's off."

Caught off guard by the vehemence in his voice, she wished she'd involved Warren the moment the phone rang. If this call had been on speakerphone, she could have had help dissecting the words or encouraging Braeden to talk. As it was, she only had her gut to trust and it told her that Braeden knew something integral to the threat against her.

Wasn't it time she started counting on herself anyway? She'd spent the past year throwing herself in front of the camera as a body double to prove she wouldn't be run out of the business and to assure herself she didn't need a negative body image. Hadn't that experience taught her some measure of self-reliance?

Acting on instinct, she capitalized on one of the few leads that might reveal a stalker, a murderer and possibly the business structure behind an underage porn ring.

"Okay." Taking a deep breath, she figured she'd set up the appointment on her own and then bring the information to Warren. If she had to back out, so be it. "Where should I meet you and when?"

"You said you're coming in from out of town?"

"Yes."

"Driving or flying?"

"I'll be driving."

"From which direction?"

"I'll be coming from the north." She didn't see any great harm in sharing that much. The stalker would know where she was coming from anyhow.

"Then I'll meet you at Ramapo rest area on the New York State Thruway. How's six o'clock? Does that give you enough time to get there?"

She could be there in less than an hour, but she didn't share that with him. Better to simply agree and let him think she could be in Canada.

"Fine."

"And, Tabitha?" His voice was abrupt, his professional tone.

"Yeah?"

"Come alone or I'll turn my car around and drive straight home." The phone disconnected on the other end, leaving Tabitha to contend with the sudden silence.

She didn't know quite how to handle this request for a private audience, but she knew she was done ducking from life and hoping the worst would be over soon. As of today, she'd find a way to take charge of her future. If that meant facing up to some unpleasant truths about her ex, she would be ready.

Warren had battled his way through a hellish childhood to become someone strong and honorable even though life had conspired against him. If he could still believe in himself and the justice system after all he'd been through, couldn't she find the strength to put her ex behind bars?

With tender new feelings for Warren curling gently around her heart, Tabitha knew the answer was a resounding yes. Because no ghosts from the past would intrude on her chance for a future with Warren.

"HE SAID HE HAD information on Manny's business dealings?"

As he sat across from Tabitha at the kitchen table, Warren tried unsuccessfully to tamp down his frustration at not being notified of this phone call the moment it came in. In her defense, Tabitha had obviously done what she thought was best by arranging a meeting with someone who had information pertinent to his investigation. But he couldn't keep her safe if she went anywhere without him, even if he sat in another car nearby.

Too risky.

"Yes." She sat rigidly on her bench at the built-in table. "I thought you'd want to know what he had to offer since Manny has been on your list of suspects from the beginning."

"I do want to know. I'm just not willing to put you at risk to find out." He debated alternate methods. "You're sure he won't talk to you on the phone? Did you offer to make a phone call on a landline? We could take you to a pay phone or reroute the call from here so it looks like it's coming from somewhere else."

She was already shaking her head, her small feather earrings dancing back and forth with the movement.

"He nixed the phone out of concern for his privacy. Maybe he thinks he could be recorded." She shrugged and the feathers rested on her shoulder for a moment before she relaxed again.

It seemed an odd time for him to notice her clothes, but the earrings led his eye on a visual journey south to the top buttons unfastened on her blouse. Even now he couldn't ignore his attraction to her.

"Recorded phone calls are probably a valid fear, given that I would have liked to do just that, but—" Damn. He didn't want to tell her all the ways she could have handled the call after the fact, but the meeting she'd set up put him in a hell of a spot.

"I'm sorry I didn't track you down during the call." Resting her chin in her elbow, she stared him down, her gaze challenging him to say the wrong thing.

No doubt she felt defensive since her ex had apparently tried his level best to chip away at her self-esteem. Didn't she expect him to do the same? The idea forced him to take a step back. Reevaluate.

"No. You did what you thought would be best. I should have prepped you for that kind of scenario. If he calls again—or if anyone else calls—just make sure you put the phone on speaker and position yourself close to me."

"Done. You're sure we shouldn't try to rearrange the meeting to another location that works for you?" She bit her lip, her worry obvious. "What if he knows something significant?"

The temptation to nail Tabitha's cheating ex was strong, but Warren wouldn't allow personal feelings to play havoc with his case. The fact that this guy Braeden had made contact with Tabitha in the first place moved the lawyer higher up the suspect list. Could the attorney be connected to the illicit films of young girls being distributed for a profit? Donata had thought all along that a legitimate film-maker had a hand in the illegal scam since the editing of the so-called reality-porn films was slick and professional.

Manny fit the bill, of course, but so did most of his friends. Both Evelyn and Braeden had been listed as assistant producers on some of his projects. Production credits were easy enough to obtain if you had some money to pour into film projects.

"Warren?" Tabitha's voice reminded him he hadn't answered her.

"Sorry. We'll revisit the matter of Braeden in a little while. First, I wonder if Manny ever used that .38 he bought you for fun or practice?"

Tabitha's eyebrows knit together. Clearly she hadn't expected to go down this road again.

"He did go to a local practice range after he bought the cursed thing. But since his monstrously large ego couldn't stand the idea of looking totally clueless at the firing range, he took the gun out in our backyard and fired at cans or a dartboard or something in the nearby woods."

Oh, that made his day.

If he could tie the murder weapon more closely to Manny Redding, the suspect list narrowed and the case would be all the easier to build. And the satisfaction of putting her ex behind bars would be all the sooner realized.

"You said you used to live in Connecticut, right?" They could make the drive in a couple of hours. He kept an old four-wheel drive truck in the garage for winter trips. They could use that since his friends had taken his car back to the city to trick the stalker.

"Yes. Why?"

"We're going to make this easier on ourselves by solving the dilemma of the murder weapon once and for all. If I can dig some shell casings out of a tree, I'll be able to tell if the weapon that shot John de Milo belonged to you."

"You can tell that?" She sounded doubtful.

He couldn't deny taking a little pride in anything that had the power to impress her. But that momentary wave crashed as the notion of the very real danger she faced chilled his soul. He wouldn't let anything happen to her. She'd shown him more empathy, more understanding about an admittedly convoluted and screwed-up past than any other woman he'd ever met. Including his wife.

No way would he let the ugliness of her ex-husband's world touch her. Not while he drew breath.

"Damn straight I can." He checked his watch as he sketched out a mental plan for how the day would unfold. "Pack up whatever you need in case we do an overnight and I'll meet you back here in ten."

She nodded, already standing. He appreciated the level of trust she gave him by agreeing to go so readily. Damn but he'd do anything to keep her safe.

"And don't forget—" He caught her arm before she headed for the stairs. "Bring your cell phone."

16

TENSION VISE-GRIPPED Tabitha's neck as they drove through her old Connecticut neighborhood and she found herself wishing for a bag of potato chips. Doughnuts. Godiva chocolates. The need for a distraction, an indulgence, left her wound-up to the point of shaking as Warren turned onto the cul de sac where she'd lived.

"You okay?" Warren's voice across the console of his pickup truck sent her old habits running for cover, the desire for potato chips disappearing when she could be fulfilled by his concern for her instead.

She reached for him. Squeezing his forearm as he downshifted. Did it make her weak to need his touch? Was she only trading one crutch for another? Logically she understood that it was healthier to need a person than to need to control her food intake. But she didn't want to put Warren in the awkward position of saving her from herself. Bad enough he'd had to protect her from a killer.

"Fine. Better than if I was by myself for this trek, that's for sure." She kept the words light on purpose, hoping to convey her appreciation without making him feel obligated. Her hand rubbed along the warm muscle of his forearm. "That's it right there."

She pointed to the house she'd moved into with so much hope once upon a time. The mammoth residence had been a tangible way for Manny to flaunt his growing wealth but Tabitha had seen it as a commitment to a quieter lifestyle outside the fishbowl of the Manhattan film industry. Too bad Manny had opted to spend most nights at their apartment in the city—without her. That should have been her fist clue.

The yard appeared more sterile than when she'd lived there since the side garden had been the one place where she'd imprinted herself, planting a wild cottage garden where flowers of all colors grew stem to stem in a pretty ramble. Manny had hated the disorganization of it and apparently the new owners hadn't thought much of it, either. Neatly pruned rosebushes had been planted in the space that used to be her cottage garden, although nothing bloomed now as the wind blew cold through the mature trees lining the dead-end street.

"This is the house of the all-white room?" Warren had stopped the car to study the place with her.

"This is the one. I bet the new owners loved it." Seeing the old place made her grateful for her small apartment with its profusion of mismatched furniture and antique scarves covering the weathered lamp shades. She'd take character over perfection any day.

"Should I park here?" Warren checked the rearview mirror and then peered around the quiet street.

"No. Manny practiced shooting in the woods at the

end of the cul de sac." She pointed to the paved circle of pavement and the dense trees behind it. "Park over there."

Five minutes later they were walking through the wooded area worth a small fortune in real estate dollars. Tabitha knew that because Manny had wanted desperately to buy the land and build on it. She couldn't remember when she realized that her ex was far more concerned with making money than with making films, but that awareness was the beginning of the end for them. When they first met he'd listened so carefully to her creative ideas, even investing in film projects she deemed strong contenders. But then he became more interested in producing than directing and he began paying attention to more important opinions than hers. She'd morphed from someone who could help his financial ends to someone who managed his household, a position she'd compromised with the cottage garden, no doubt.

Oddly, the realization soothed some of the old anguish she'd felt about his affair. She'd lashed out at Evelyn because she hadn't understood where else to cast blame for her unhappiness, but now she saw the way she'd conspired in her own divorce. Her lack of awareness about what made her happy left her an easy target for someone with Manny's carefully applied charm.

"We should be getting closer," she called out to Warren as she tromped over a fallen branch at the top of a short hill.

Sunlight permeated the woods despite the dense trees since the branches were still bare. A few patches of snow dotted the ground in low places. Tabitha hadn't ever walked down here with Manny since she'd wanted nothing to do with the gun and she knew there were local ordinances against firing a weapon in an area with residential buildings so close by. But she'd taken refuge in the trees at other times while Manny was at work, the natural setting making her worldly problems seem small and unimportant. On one of those outings—the day she'd waited for a taxi to pick her up the morning after she'd discovered Manny's affair—she'd noticed the tree riddled with shell casings from target practice.

"Bingo." Warren's shout from a few feet away caused her to turn.

"That's it." She spotted the tree that had caught his eye and she watched him pull on gloves to sift through the dead leaves at the base of the maple.

Her stomach lurched at the idea they could be collecting evidence to prove Manny was far worse than a cheating husband. Could she have been married to a killer all those years? The corn muffin she'd had for breakfast churned uncomfortably in her belly.

"Can you tell anything just by looking at it?" She wondered how long they'd have to wait for an answer.

"Nothing definitive." His search under the tree seemed to come up empty so he went to work extracting a slug from the trunk. "We can't be certain without some lab work, but if there's a mark on this casing that looks similar to the one we collected from the murder scene and from your apartment—"

He broke off as the bit of metal came free from the trunk of the tree. The casing glistened dully in the sunlight as he held it at the end of a tool that looked like long, industrial-strength tweezers. Turning the bullet around, Warren studied every angle.

"Well?" Her heart stuttered at a silence that seemed too long. Too pregnant with meaning.

"I have to collect a few more so we have a thorough sampling." He swung his gaze her way. "But my first impression is that Manny's gun definitely killed de Milo."

WARREN HADN'T EXPECTED the news to be easy to take. He knew how devastating it could be to find out that someone you loved and trusted possessed the ability to take a human life. Memories from his first screaming match with the officer who arrested Andy came floating back to him now as Tabitha wobbled unsteadily on her feet.

"I can't have been married to a murderer." Her breathy voice sounded close to hyperventilating as he tugged a second casing out of the tree.

"You might not have been." He regretted the need to bring her here, but he couldn't have left her behind. Not after what had happened last time.

"What do you mean?" Pacing around the trees while he worked, Tabitha finally sat down on a dead stump of a fallen tree.

"Just because it was Manny's gun doesn't mean he fired it, remember?" Warren knew that her ex's girlfriend could have access to the weapon, but he should have reminded her of that before she panicked at the thought of Manny being a killer.

Still, Warren couldn't help but think her ex had the

best case for being bitter about their split. No matter that he'd been the one to cheat on her. This guy's identity seemed bound up in his ego and Tabitha's public denouncing of him had obviously hit him between the eyes.

Or maybe Warren just hated the guy because he'd hurt a woman Warren had grown to care about. A lot. There was a chance Warren's anger was as tied up in this case as Manny's ego was tied to his image.

"If you think there's a better chance that Manny is the—" she swallowed "—the guy you're looking for, don't you think we ought to keep the appointment I set with Braeden tonight?"

"Braeden could have accessed Manny's gun if the two were friends." He remembered Tabitha saying they'd maintained their friendship long after Braeden's ex-girlfriend had hooked up with Manny. But what motive would Braeden have for the stalking crime that seemed too personal? It would be one thing for the guy to stalk his ex. But Tabitha had been as duped by Manny and Evelyn as Braeden had.

"But you don't think Braeden took the gun, do you?" Tabitha seemed to read his mind as he dropped the last shell casing into a bag for evidence.

"I think we need to go into the city so I can get to my lab anyway. If we pull some backup for the meeting with Braeden, I guess it couldn't hurt to hear what he has to say." Warren wouldn't be taking any risks where Tabitha was concerned until they had their suspect in custody.

His feelings for her had expanded and grown in ways he hadn't anticipated this week, but from the shock etched in her gaze, he suspected she wouldn't be in a place to return those feelings anytime soon. Just his luck that the one time he was finally able to put aside his past long enough to really connect with someone, her past had to rear up and deliver a knockout punch like this. Finding out your ex was allegedly capable of murder would sour anyone on relationships.

Anger hovered over him like a black cloud as he shoved the evidence bag into his jacket pocket. He stalked around a tree to get to Tabitha when the sound of gunfire cracked through the woods.

TABITHA THOUGHT she'd lost it when Warren announced that Manny's gun had killed porn star de Milo. But the minibreakdown she'd experienced in the woods at that time couldn't compare to the heart failure she was going through in the passenger seat of Warren's truck as they raced out of Connecticut at a high speed, a siren propped in the dash to let traffic see the law enforcement affiliation.

Holy crap.

Her heart slammed into her ribs in erratic explosions, each beat making her whole body reverberate in response while Warren radioed in the incident to his dispatcher. Or maybe it was a local police dispatcher. She had no idea.

"I don't see anybody behind us." Warren's voice still sounded tense, but he spoke more softly now that he'd set down the handset to the police radio.

They were only scant miles from the woods and Tabitha froze as she realized someone might be following. If anything, that's what Warren had been expecting

since they were doing ninety miles an hour up the interstate across the state border into New York. Somehow,
she'd thought they'd escaped the worst when they'd made
it into the safety of the car after a shot had pierced the air.

"But you thought we weren't being followed when
we left the Catskills this morning." She didn't mean to
give him a hard time, but fear made her mouth run fast
as the scenery whipped past in a blur. "I just mean—"

"I know what you mean," he said tersely. "And while
a car may possibly be following without me knowing,
there's probably a better chance there's another tracking
device planted in the truck."

She tried not to look at the speedometer that nudged
over ninety miles an hour.

"How could—"

"Remember how the motion detectors went off the
other night?" Finally slowing down, he steered the car
off the highway to an exit ramp. "Someone could have
dropped a device in the vehicle then. We already knew
there was someone lurking around the property, right?"

She remembered Warren's neighbor had called the
cops about the stranger's car parked nearby.

"So what do we do now?" She couldn't staunch the
urge to look out the rear windshield, convinced her ex-
husband would be barreling down on them in his Audi.
No, wait. His neighbor said she'd seen a white sedan.
Had to be a rental car.

"We're going to comb through the vehicle to see if
we find anything and get something else to drive. Then
we're getting a warrant for Manny Redding and bring-

ing his girlfriend and his former attorney in for questioning."

"Okay. Yes. Under arrest is good." She scoped out the gas station they seemed to be heading for. "Assuming we can find him before he…you know…shoots me. Or you."

Her voice croaked on that last note and she regretted dragging him into the mess of her life.

"We're going to be fine. Nothing will happen to either of us." He spoke with stern authority when he had no way of ensuring that a bullet didn't hit him during his self-imposed guardianship. But then, his thoughts seemed a million miles away as he ducked into an open service bay while the station attendant yelled at them to back out.

"But if I hadn't been hiding from life for the last year, maybe I would have seen that my husband was involved in something illegal." The reality that he could be peddling underage porn along with the other host of crimes still hadn't fully sunk in. And oh, God, how could she have missed something so evil?

Anger burned away some of the fear she'd felt back in the woods as Warren jumped out of the car and flashed his badge at the attendant. In quick response, the manager lowered the garage door to hide their truck from the street while two other mechanics circled the vehicle, looking at her curiously.

Feeling strangely disconnected from what was happening, Tabitha slid out of the truck and backed out of the garage through a second open bay. Warren juggled a phone in one hand while he went through the truck bed with the other.

He looked so strong. Vital. She couldn't fathom this dynamic, capable man falling victim to one of the bullets he'd made it his mission to study, but when all was said and done his body could be pierced as easily and as lethally as anyone else's.

She'd backed so far from the hubbub in the garage that her butt suddenly hit a gas pump, startling her. In a minute she would go back inside and join the search for a tracking device but right this moment she needed to gather her strength to combat the surreal quality of this day. She wouldn't be weak with Warren the way she'd been weak—blind—with Manny.

She refused to go through another relationship telling herself over and over that everything would be okay when it wouldn't. Her marriage hadn't been okay, and damn it, Warren wouldn't come through this in one piece just because she willed it.

"Tabitha."

The sound of her name dawned like the censuring voice of her conscience. She startled a step and then realized that Braeden O'Leary had pulled up alongside her in a dark blue BMW.

Did he know his former best friend was probably a killer? Could he have the information that would prove it and put Manny behind bars?

"Braeden." She tried to process his presence there. Were they close to the New York State Thruway? Judging by the thick traffic on the interstate, maybe six o'clock wasn't that far off.

"You headed to our meeting point?" He had a map

spread out on his dashboard. "It's only a couple of miles but I ran out of gas."

Were they really that close to their meeting place? She'd lost all sense of time and direction during their high-speed flight out of her old neighborhood, but she supposed they'd covered some distance given that they were going ninety or a hundred miles an hour at one point. Maybe they were close to Tarrytown but it was tough to tell with all the smaller towns north of the city blending into an endless chain of strip malls.

Glancing toward the garage, she wondered how to convince Braeden to conduct the meeting at the police station, but as she turned back to him, she realized he was opening the passenger side door.

Near her.

She meant to step back but her sluggish brain was still stuck on a truckload of scattered thoughts from the last hour. Before she could react, Braeden yanked her arm down and sideways with brutal force.

She screamed then, recognition penetrating her gray matter at the same time the stick shift jabbed into her temple. The car lurched forward, her feet still hanging out the door.

Tires squealed in time with her hoarse shout until the stick shift jammed down into another gear and knocked her in the teeth. She had a last vision of the gray March sky and telephone poles whipping past the windshield. Then a noxious odor on a damp white cloth filled her nose and mouth. Her senses rebelled, sickened. She arched back away from it, a seat belt buckle biting into her head.

Her last thought before her senses caved to the drug was that Warren didn't get to see the face of the man who took her.

17

BRAEDEN "RED" O'LEARY had always been a man who prided himself on his ability to remain quietly grounded in a business full of high-strung personalities. He negotiated good deals for his clients by keeping his cool. And he'd recently discovered that he understood the justice system so well that he could eliminate his enemies without getting caught. The successful dispatch of John de Milo proved it since de Milo knew about Braeden's tie to the black market company called Red Light District—a front for lucrative underage porn.

And now thanks to a stolen weapon and a few tracking devices he'd be able to eliminate Tabitha Everhart as easily. She might not have remembered their long-ago cocktail party conversation in which he'd questioned her about the porn industry her husband had worked in for years, but there was no telling when the information might rise to the surface. Especially now that she had an NYPD detective sharing her bed 24/7.

And admittedly, today's scene at the gas station hadn't been his best work. Braeden couldn't figure out what the hell was wrong with him that he couldn't pull off a simple grab-and-dash without creating a big ruckus.

He looked down at his unconscious companion in the front seat of the BMW and wondered what to do with her as he sat at the pull-off before the Tappan Zee Bridge. He'd planned to simply dump her off the bridge after nightfall and be done with her since the fall alone would kill her. But considering all the ways he'd messed up with Tabitha so far, he had to wonder if that was a bad idea and he just wasn't seeing it.

She was such a sweet person. So much better than Manny Redding had ever deserved. How unfortunate that she couldn't have just walked away from her ex-husband without creating so much of a media circus, drawing an excruciating amount of attention to Manny's life, and eventually, Braeden's. The divorce had forced Braeden to slow down his moneymaking film pursuits for months while he represented his supposed best friend in the split. It soothed Braeden's ego on numerous levels to frame Manny for de Milo's murder and now Tabitha's. He'd chosen the stalking route purposely to add dramatic flair to the crime and cinch Manny as a suspect since Manny had stopped funding Braeden's reality-porn flicks. Manny had been fine with the whole endeavor, even running a few of the premises by Tabitha for storyboard advice when they first started out, but he'd gotten cold feet when Braeden started experimenting with younger stars for his straight-to-video gold mine.

Tabitha stirred in her seat and Braeden debated using more of the drug to tide her over until it was fully dark.

Then again, wasn't it close enough? The perpetual gray of March meant it was barely light out anyway and commuter traffic had come and gone. No sense waiting.

Braeden had operations to resume since the loose ends of Manny and Tabitha were soon to be tied up—the last people who could possibly implicate him in his sideline business.

"Come on, princess," he whispered to Tabitha as he wrapped an arm around her waist. "Time to wake up."

THE BASTARD had lost his goddamn mind.

Warren watched Manny's attorney friend step out of the BMW from a few hundred yards away. After following the vehicle here, Warren crouched beside the front tire of his pickup truck, the back windshield busted after he'd plowed through a half-closed garage door to follow the vehicle with Tabitha inside.

Backup was nearby, but the light could be tricky on the high bridge with the way fog lingered around the structure this time of year, making a sniper shot risky as hell on a bridge that saw nonstop traffic. Snow melted off the cliffs during the warmer days and then hung in white clouds suspended at the level of the bridge, making visibility suck all around. Maybe that's why Braeden O'Leary thought he could get away with bringing Tabitha here despite the public venue. Mostly, Warren figured the guy had lost his marbles.

Adrenaline blasted through him with turbo speed, making Warren's legs itch to run and tackle the guy. But he didn't want to spook a man who was barely holding on to sanity, so he opted to take measured steps along the railing of a bridge famed for its jumpers.

Tabitha.

The thought of her being shoved off the structure at gunpoint propelled Warren's feet faster in spite of himself. Logically, he knew stealth and surprise would be the best way to take this guy down.

Bloodlust urged him to get his hands around O'Leary's throat as fast as possible.

The unassuming-looking attorney walked coolly over to the passenger side of his vehicle, which was parked far from any streetlamp. He pulled open the door and reached down into the passenger seat where Warren was certain Tabitha waited. God, he hoped she'd waited.

His gut dropped when he saw O'Leary have to help her from the car, her body limp. His legs quickened their pace even as he missed a step out of ice-cold fear.

Warren's eyes stung as he focused on Tabitha's slumped form. He'd only taken his eyes off her for a second in that garage, but he never thought she'd get that far away from him....

He'd never forgive himself if something happened to the one woman who didn't condemn him for his past and didn't expect him to pretend it never happened.

Sweat rolled down Warren's back as he neared O'Leary's BMW. The sound of traffic hid the noise of his feet on the asphalt as he passed one bridge support after another on the seemingly endless causeway leading up to the heart of the bridge. And damn it, why did he have to remember with sudden, stupid clarity this bridge was one hundred and thirty-eight feet high? He banished the number from his head and kept moving. Faster.

Was she okay? Could this bastard have been stupid enough to hurt her in a car where he'd leave behind all the evidence in the world? Warren knew he'd take no satisfaction out of locking the guy up for the rest of his life. If Tabitha was…

Jesus.

If O'Leary damaged one red hair on her perfect head, the guy would hit the Hudson like a ton of bricks after Warren was done with him.

Gun drawn, he dove between Tabitha and O'Leary. He had a brief impression of her body being warm as his arm brushed her shoulder on the way to the ground. He wrestled with O'Leary, using his gun to crack him in the head before the weapon skittered out of his grip and across the tarmac to teeter between the trusses of the bridge before the long fall down.

Not that he needed the weapon. The visual of Tabitha crumpling to the ground in his peripheral vision provided all the ammunition Warren needed to kill this guy with his bare hands. Fury lit his fists as he landed a blow to O'Leary's gut. His temple. His—

"Warren."

Tabitha's voice halted him, the sound a croak of life from a few feet away since he knew damn well it wasn't his conscience talking. Hope swamped him heavier than the mist hanging over the bridge.

"Tabitha?" He released O'Leary and scrambled over to her, wondering when the hell his backup would arrive. Seconds counted when a bullet could end a life in less than an instant.

"He's got Manny's gun." She tried to lift her head but couldn't. He didn't see any blood on her but she had a nasty bruise on her cheek as if a shaft of metal had come in contact with her face.

Panic assaulted him all over again. Had she been beaten? Warren knew a beating could kill a person quietly after the blows had been exchanged. His brother had come close once after their father had been drinking.

"Are you okay?" He reached her side, cradling her head in his hands as footsteps drew closer and police shouted at O'Leary to put his hands up.

Thank God. Thank God. Thank you, God.

"Fine. Drugs." She opened her eyes for a split second but the pupils rolled back again and she closed her lids. "Don't drop him over the side. He's got Manny's gun."

She hadn't been beaten. Drugs were making her sluggish. Relief flooded his veins. Why was the gun so important to her? All he could care about right this minute was that she was all right. Warm. Alive.

In his arms where she belonged.

"I know he took the gun," he assured her, although he wished like hell he'd known it a few days earlier.

He nodded to Donata Casale, the detective who'd been tracking the underage porn case long before Warren had gotten involved. She took charge of the scene as cop cars screeched into place to form a barrier around the action at the rail.

"I didn't want you to drown good evidence." Tabitha spoke with her eyes closed, but a smile pulled at her lips.

His heart stuttered in his chest and he knew right then he was more vulnerable to this woman than he'd ever been to any woman. Hell, the roller-coaster ride he'd been on for the last hour told him he'd keep being vulnerable to Tabitha for the rest of his life.

For just one more moment he savored the feel of her, the scent of her. All his.

"We'll string the bastard up by his toenails, I promise." O'Leary had started making some major errors in the last twenty-four hours and Warren was positive the evidence would show as much. But Tabitha was right. Having the murder weapon in his possession was going to make this case all the easier to finalize.

"I want to go home now," she mumbled into his jacket, her body still awkward after whatever drug she'd been given. "I have to let Buster out."

Warren smiled, knowing they'd left the dog in the basement of his house in the Catskills. Could that be where she wanted to go? Home with him?

The surge of possessiveness he felt seemed so right. So meant-to-be.

Picking her up as carefully as he'd gather sensitive evidence, he navigated his way through the crowd of cops and cars toward the undercover vehicle. With no need to worry about being followed or shot at, he could take his time and treat this incredible woman the way she deserved to be treated. He just prayed when the drugs wore off she was as happy to see him as he was to have her back.

Because there wasn't a chance in hell he could let her go now.

TABITHA DOVE BACK into the bed in Warren's guest suite at the Catskills house two days later, determined that her surly caretaker wouldn't find her out of bed. She had a kick-ass surprise for him she didn't want to ruin.

"What are you doing?" He glared at her with suspicion in his dark eyes, his gaze raking over the covers she'd pulled up to her neck. "The doc said you were supposed to rest, remember?"

"For twenty-four hours." She tried not to roll her eyes since she sort of appreciated having someone care about her health, even though his vigilance was taking a serious toll on her sex life today. "Lucky for you I'm all better and ready to show you something I made."

He scowled at her with the same fierce glance he'd had etched on his face for two days straight. Part of the problem was that she'd probably scared him to death when the drug Braeden gave her made her appear fatally wounded. But she suspected the other part of the problem was that Warren had a hard time cutting himself any slack in life and he somehow blamed himself for her stupidity in walking out of the garage at the service station where Braeden had snatched her.

As if.

She hadn't found the right words to convince him he couldn't take on the whole world's problems or make up for everyone else's cluelessness, but she was hoping her special gift would help.

"I brought you here to get well, not to tax yourself with—"

"Sit." She cleared a spot on the bed beside her, swiping aside pillows with her bare arm, the only part of herself she allowed to slide out of the covers.

"I don't think—" He stared at her bare shoulder in a way that made her think she wouldn't be sex-starved for too much longer.

Pleasurable anticipation filtered through her veins like warm honey.

"Come on." She pulled on his arm with one hand as she reached beneath the covers with the other to retrieve the remote control. "I found your video camera in the linen closet and thought I'd reacquaint myself with my filmmaking skills in preparation for my next documentary."

The antiquated equipment had given her low-quality footage, but the craftsmanship required to film the short piece had ignited passions she'd squelched for far too long.

"You made a film?" He sat beside her, propping one leg on the bed as he glanced back and forth between her and the television set occupying an antique armoire.

At last she had him in her bed. *Victory.*

She wanted to celebrate since he'd found out he wouldn't be facing any disciplinary action from a professional review committee. He'd received a warning from his chief in the form of a lengthy closed-door talk.

Warren had thought the end result was fair. Especially since he didn't plan to repeat the trend with any other women he met through his job. Tabitha liked hearing that.

"Yes, I made a film. It will be the first of many with any luck. I don't care how many editing jobs I have to take to wheedle my way back into that end of the business. Sooner or later I'm going to be sitting in the creative director's chair."

Hearing what Warren had overcome to be the amazing man he was made her realize she would never get ahead reaching out with tentative, shaking fingers. It was time to leave the pity party of the past behind and grasp her future with both hands.

She'd forgotten how much she loved filmmaking, the piece of herself she'd let go in an effort to keep her marriage together.

Why hadn't she realized that no relationship could work if you weren't being true to yourself first? Thankfully, being with Warren had reminded her of the kind of person she wanted to be. She felt healthier and happier with him than she had been in years. Maybe her whole life. She'd realized how much she cared about him in those agonizing moments where she thought O'Leary might kill her. Amazing how quickly priorities could realign when you were confronted with the possibility you might not wake up in the morning.

Pressing Play, she was surprised when Warren's hand covered hers, pausing the track before it could begin.

"They brought Manny in for questioning today." His eyes locked with hers as if gauging her reaction.

"I'm hoping he can help build the case against Braeden?" She knew they had Braeden for murder and for attempted murder. But he'd been guilty of so much more with his films. "The girls who appeared in his films without their knowledge deserve to see justice served. His part in packaging and distributing underage reality-porn tore apart lots of lives."

"Manny knew Braeden financed some low-budget films a few years ago. He said you did, too?" There was no suspicion in his voice, only a desire for confirmation.

She snuggled deeper under the covers of the four-poster bed in the house she loved for its clean simplicity. The chenille bedspread rubbed her chin with soft welcome. Buster paced outside and it occurred to her that Warren had thoughtfully closed the door.

A very good sign.

"Yes, I know. Manny financed those kinds of films, too, at one point. But once he got on board with the soap opera, he only did more legitimate pictures." She hoped Warren didn't think badly of her because she'd offered up suggestions for improving the crappy dialogue in a couple of erotic films targeted toward horny men. "And Manny never hired underage actresses."

"That's what he said. Apparently the final straw that broke the friendship wasn't Evelyn leaving Braeden for Manny, but that Manny knew Braeden was hiring younger and younger stars."

"But knowingly distributing footage of teens showing off on their webcams is a far cry from accidentally hiring an actress who lies about her age."

Warren's shoulders relaxed. "I just wanted to bring you up to speed on the case."

"I'm glad." She was just so relieved that Manny hadn't been trying to kill her. Her ex was a jerk, but he wasn't a killer and he didn't promote underage porn.

Thank you, God.

Her faith in her judgment had been restored a little. And damn it, being with Warren had shaken her out of the numb acceptance of life she'd fallen into after her divorce. She was ready to embrace her dreams again.

Smiling up at him, she refrained from throwing herself into his arms and settled for pressing the play button on the remote. If all went well she hoped there would be time for throwing herself in his arms later. She hoped she hadn't misread the signs of his interest, too—an interest that went beyond a simple one-night stand.

"Holy—" His eyes widened as he watched the screen, his attention thoroughly hooked by the image of her dancing around the bedroom in a negligee with a silk scarf wound around her head like an Arabian princess.

"I thought I'd start off small scale by just concentrating on developing key scenes for artistic variety and sharp content." She timed her words against the backdrop of her hooking a leg around the bedpost in the video, her thigh showcased in the optimal light to make her look more muscular. There were definite benefits to creating your own seductive video when you'd attended film school.

Lighting 101 could make a woman look sexier than the best makeup job in the world.

"Tabitha, you know I can't watch this and then walk away." His expression appeared so comically anguished she couldn't smother a giggle.

"That's the point," she whispered in his ear, letting her tongue flick over his neck. "I want you to touch me afterward."

"You're so bruised." He tore his gaze away from the video with an effort to check the purple skin around her cheek and temple.

"The ache between my thighs is much more urgent, I swear." She captured his hand and drew it down the front of her body, still wrapped in the gauzy scarf that was actually one of her long skirts cut into pieces.

"You're incredible," he whispered hoarsely, diving beneath the covers to expose the rest of her.

She had the feeling the rest of her little video would go unwatched, but that was okay. She'd save the strip-tease footage for tomorrow.

"I just want to be with you." She wrenched his T-shirt up over his chest, grateful he'd taken a week's vacation to help her recover. She suddenly felt the need for a great deal of tending.

"I'm not going anywhere," he reminded her, his eyes meeting hers with a fierce heat that assured her he would be as passionate about keeping her close as he'd been about keeping his distance at first.

She wouldn't push him for words of love and commitment even if she felt them deep inside her soul already, but she knew they were ready to take the first steps into a future together.

"Then touch me," she urged, so ready for more she could barely lay still.

"Promise me you're going to move in with me first." He eased the remote out of her hand as he pinned her wrists to the bed, dominating her gently but oh-so-well.

Everything inside her went still as she processed what he was asking. For Warren, this seemed like a huge leap forward.

"Really?" She hadn't expected him to be ready for that much of a first step, but the idea had definite appeal for a woman who wanted to see him and touch him during every spare moment of their lives.

Living together would be a very, very good thing.

"Oh, yeah. But only if it feels right to you." His thigh eased its way between her legs, her sex shielded by nothing more than the whisper-thin fabric of her long scarf.

This definitely felt right. Clear down to her toes. She shivered in response.

"You make a hell of a convincing argument, Detective." Arching her back, she rubbed her breasts against his chest, gladly playing along with this game.

"Is that a yes?" His head dipped to trail kisses along her shoulder to the curve of her neck.

Chills broke out over her skin and heat flooded her insides as she thought of all the ways they could explore each others' bodies if they had unlimited time together.

As she considered all the time they could spend learning about each other and sharing popcorn over corny movies where people actually wore clothes.

"That's a definite yes. A resounding yes."

His kiss answered her in a thousand ways until she gave herself over to heated visions of a future with this incredible, sexy man.

For now, that was more than enough. In fact, she couldn't imagine anything more perfect.

* * * * *

Turn the page for a sneak preview of
IF I'D NEVER KNOWN YOUR LOVE
by
Georgia Bockoven

From the brand-new series
Harlequin Everlasting Love
Every great love has a story to tell. ™

There's no way for you to know this, Evan, but I haven't written to you for a few months. Actually, it's been almost a year. I had a hard time picking up a pen once more after we paid the second ransom and then received a letter saying it wasn't enough. I was so sure you were coming home that I took the kids along to Bogotá so they could fly home with you and me, something I swore I'd never do. I've fallen in love with Colombia and the people who've opened their hearts to me. But fear is a constant companion when I'm there. I won't ever expose our children to that kind of danger again.

I'm at a loss over what to do anymore, Evan. I've begged and pleaded and thrown temper tantrums with every official I can corner both here and at home. They've been incredibly tolerant and understanding, but in the end as ineffectual as the rest of us.

I try to imagine what your life is like now, what you do every day, what you're wearing, what you eat. I want to believe that the people who have you are misguided yet kind, that they treat you well. It's how I survive day to day. To think of you being mistreated hurts too much. If I picture you locked away somewhere and suffering, a weight descends on me that makes it almost impossible to get out of bed in the morning.

Your captors surely know you by now. They have to recognize what a good man you are. I imagine you working with their children, telling them that you have children, too, showing them the pictures you carry in your wallet. Can't the men who have you understand how much your children miss you? How can it not matter to them?

How can they keep you away from us all this time? Over and over, we've done what they asked. Are they oblivious to the depth of their cruelty? What kind of people are they that they don't care?

I used to keep a calendar beside our bed next to the peach rose you picked for me before you left. Every night I marked another day, counting how many you'd been gone. I don't do that any longer. I don't want to be reminded of all the days we'll never get back.

When I can't sleep at night, I tell you about my day. I imagine you hearing me and smiling over the details that make up my life now. I never tell you how defeated I feel at moments or how hard I work to hide it from everyone for fear they will see it as a reason to stop believing you are coming home to us.

And I couldn't tell you about the lump I found in my breast and how difficult it was going through all the tests without you here to lean on. The lump was benign—the process reaching that diagnosis utterly terrifying. I couldn't stop thinking about what would happen to Shelly and Jason if something happened to me.

We need you to come home.

I'm worn down with missing you.

I'm going to read this tomorrow and will probably tear it up or burn it in the fireplace. I don't want you to get the idea I ever doubted what I was doing to free you or thought the work a burden. I would gladly spend the rest of my life at it, even if, in the end, we only had one day together.

You are my life, Evan.

I will love you forever.

* * * * *

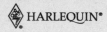

HARLEQUIN® *Romance*®

presents a brand-new trilogy by

PATRICIA THAYER

Rocky Mountain BRIDES

Three sisters come home to wed.

In April don't miss
Raising the Rancher's Family,

followed by
The Sheriff's Pregnant Wife,
on sale May 2007,

and
A Mother for the Tycoon's Child,
on sale June 2007.

Silhouette®

Romantic
SUSPENSE

Excitement, danger and passion guaranteed!

USA TODAY bestselling author
Marie Ferrarella
is back with the second installment
in her popular miniseries,
*The Doctors Pulaski: Medicine
just got more interesting...*
DIAGNOSIS: DANGER is on sale
April 2007 from Silhouette®
Romantic Suspense (formerly
Silhouette Intimate Moments).

*Look for it wherever
you buy books!*

REQUEST YOUR FREE BOOKS!

2 FREE NOVELS PLUS 2 FREE GIFTS!

HARLEQUIN®

Blaze

Red-hot reads!

Introducing talented new author

TESSA RADLEY

*making her Silhouette Desire debut
this April with*

BLACK WIDOW BRIDE

Book #1794
Available in April 2007.

Wealthy Damon Asteriades had no choice but to
force Rebecca Grainger back to his family's estate—
despite his vow to keep away from her seductive
charms. But being so close to the woman society once
dubbed the Black Widow Bride had him aching to
claim her as his own...at any cost.

On sale April from Silhouette Desire!

**Available wherever books are sold,
including most bookstores, supermarkets,
discount stores and drugstores.**

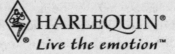

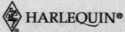

HARLEQUIN®

Blaze™

COMING NEXT MONTH

#315 COMING UNDONE Stephanie Tyler

There's a bad boy in camouflage knocking at Carly Winters's door, and she knows she's in trouble. The erotic fax that Jonathon "Hunt" Huntington's waving in her face—she can explain; how the buff Navy SEAL got ahold of it—she can't. But she sure wants to find out!

#316 SEX AS A SECOND LANGUAGE Jamie Sobrato
Lust in Translation, Bk. 1

Ariel Turner's sexual tour of Europe has landed her in Italy seeking the perfect Italian lover. But despite the friendliness of the locals, she's not having much luck. Until the day the very hot Marc Sorrella sits beside her. Could it be she's found the ideal candidate?

#317 THE HAUNTING Hope Tarr
Extreme

History professor Maggie Holliday's new antebellum home has everything she's ever wanted—including the ghost of Captain Ethan O'Malley, a Union soldier who insists Maggie's the reincarnation of his lost love. And after one incredibly sexual night in his arms, she's inclined to believe him....

#318 AT HIS FINGERTIPS Dawn Atkins
Doing it...Better! Bk. 3

When a fortune-teller predicts the return of a man from her past, Esmeralda McElroy doesn't expect Mitch Margolin. The sexy sizzle is still between them, but he's a lot more cautious than she remembers. Does this mean she'll have to seduce him to his senses?

#319 BAD BEHAVIOR Kristin Hardy
Sex & the Supper Club II, Bk. 3

Dominick Gordon can't believe it. He thinks his eyes are playing tricks on him when he spots the older, but no less beautiful, Delaney Phillips—it's been almost twenty years since they dated as teenagers. Still, Dom's immediate feelings show he's all man, and Delaney's all woman....

#320 ALL OVER YOU Sarah Mayberry
Secret Lives of Daytime Divas, Bk. 2

The last thing scriptwriter Grace Wellington wants is for the man of her fantasies to step into her life. But Mac Harrison, in his full, gorgeous glory, has done exactly that. Worse, they're now working together. That is, if Grace can keep her hands to herself!

www.eHarlequin.com   HBCNM0307